Tales of the

The Vernal S

On a warm spring day in the 1950s, twelve-year-old Jason, an only child who lives in the Midlands, arrives for a holiday in a small seaside village where his father lived as a child. Staying with an uncle and aunt, he plans to explore the rocks at low tide which his father remembers from his childhood. Soon, he meets Joe, an old man who once was an expert fisher of the shores. Joe becomes a mentor for the boy as he can describe, from memory, the exact layout of the rocks and all their secrets. When he starts to investigate the shoreline, shy Jason meets Abby, a lively young Australian girl. As their friendship grows, she comes to realise that he has a secret in his past and is escaping from something he'd rather not talk about. With more confidence, Jason becomes adept at catching prawns, crabs and even a lobster. Yet, he encounters unexpected trouble, even in these beautiful places, and will have to draw on his new resources to confront unwanted obstacles ahead...

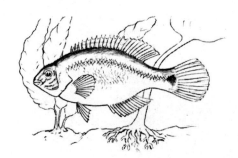

For Belle and Hugo

C D Pressdee

TALES OF THE TIDES

The Vernal Springs

AUSTIN MACAULEY PUBLISHERS™

LONDON ∗ CAMBRIDGE ∗ NEW YORK ∗ SHARJAH

A CIP catalogue record for this title is available from the British Library.

ISBN 9781528987820 (Paperback)
ISBN 9781528987837 (ePub e-book)

www.austinmacauley.com

First Published 2022
Austin Macauley Publishers Ltd®
1 Canada Square
Canary Wharf
London
E14 5AA

With great thanks to Paul Llewellyn for providing the sketches of the seashore flora and fauna. We spent many childhood hours scouring the rocks together.

To Carwyn Evans for formatting the script; Mark Nolan of Decoder for the cover design; Jamie Pressdee for the cover photograph, and the late Celeste Mitchell for assisting with editing.

Table of Contents

'Two thirds of our planet is covered by the sea; two thirds of our planet remains largely undiscovered.' Hans Hass

Barnacles

Chapter One

Oyster Catchers and a Turnstone

The First View

On a sunny springtime Tuesday afternoon, a red double-decker bus arrives in the centre of a small coastal village. A young boy peers out of the front upper window, staring in awe at the lapping waves on the sweeping shingle beach. He jumps up and darts down the stairs, pulling from under them a brown leather suitcase together with a new heart-shaped prawning net. It has never seen the sea before and neither has he. He stands back for the other passengers then steps off, walks across the square to the sea wall and gazes down at the birds scampering along the shoreline and darting from the swashing waves. A large seagull pecks at a fish head, guarding it aggressively from juvenile gulls.

A few yards away, two weather-beaten men, one large with a florid face, the other with a wizened lean visage, are chatting away. Suddenly, they stop and both glare at the boy.

'Going fishin'?' the slighter man asks.

The boy smiles. 'Yes, that's my plan. Where is the best place around here?' he asks politely.

'The sea!' comes a curt reply. His friend sniggers then they continue their banter, gazing out to sea and ignoring the young lad.

Taken aback, the boy looks up to the clear blue sky where many birds are gliding majestically on the spring thermals. In the distance, the silky blue sea dissipates into a hazy horizon.

'Master Jason?' a soft friendly voice then calls out. The boy looks around to see a sturdy man of medium height in green corduroy trousers and a slightly baggy Harris Tweed jacket walking towards him. He holds out his arms in a friendly welcome. 'I'm your Uncle Charles. Not seen ye since a child, but welcome. Your first time to the seaside, to be sure. See ye've come ready to some fishin', or prawnin' at least.'

Uncle Charles looks at Jason's excited face. The boy's complexion is healthy and unblemished and his eyes are blue and bright. A breeze ruffles his light brown hair which is neatly parted on the left.

'Hello, Uncle! Thank you for coming to meet me. Do you live far from here?'

'Just up ye hill. Come, I'll take the case; ye carry the net.'

'No, no, I'll manage. I carried it from the house all the way to the station at eight this morning. It's not too heavy, honest,' Jason says, eagerly picking it up.

'Aunty Gertie is preparing a special tea. Thought ye'd be hungry.'

'That sounds wonderful,' says Jason. 'Thank you! Do you know those two men who were on the sea wall?'

Uncle chuckles. 'Yes, both were trawler men. The little fellow is called Skipper Jonny, the other is a crew man known as Nutmeg. Rough old devils. I'll tell ye about them later, and many others here. Come on, tea will be ready.'

Charming men, Jason thinks to himself. *I hope they are not all like that.*

Together, they march briskly up a hill that leads out of the square, passing a row of shops either side, then turn left into a narrower street. Jason looks back and can now see across the bay where a few small fishing boats are drifting on the tide. In the distance, several larger ships seem to hover motionless in the haze. Beyond, on the far side of the bay, are larger buildings straddling the port area of the large industrial town that's huddled under rolling green hills. It's all so different from home, Jason thinks, and his excitement increases.

Ahead of them, a slim, elegant lady in a smart knitted dress suit is standing on the steps leading to a small semi-detached village house. She opens her arms and clasps both of Jason's hands just as he puts down the case and net.

'I was told you're a very smart young man, little Jason, what a fine green blazer that is! Come in, darling and have some tea. You must certainly be tired after such an early start,' Aunty Gertie says in a most welcoming tone. 'We want this to be a truly wonderful holiday for you. Three weeks is a long-time off school!'

'Hello, Aunty. Thank you so much for inviting me. This village is so very different from home. Yes, it is a long holiday because of the late Easter but we will only have two days at Whitsun,' Jason explains. At the same time, he is thinking what a cultured lady his Aunty seems to be, such a contrast to the two rude trawler men.

'I do hope you will like your room,' she says as she shows him up the staircase to a small bedroom. Jason's face lights up when he sees the view of the bay beyond rooftops. The sea has some areas of darker colour from currents of the flooding tide. Aunty Gertie smiles as he is transfixed by all this; it's something he's never seen before.

'Oh, yes, it's very beautiful,' she says. 'But don't be deceived by the tranquillity today; there are times when it's violent, rough and unwelcoming to all. Many a ship, sailor and swimmer have come to grief on this coast! You really must learn quickly to have the greatest respect for the sea, because when it turns nasty it's like a bully and crushes anything in its path.'

Jason starts at the word *bully* and looks a little perplexed. She smiles. 'I think you need a treat after your journey. Come downstairs.'

Jason follows Aunty into the parlour where a small hexagonal table is set neatly with a tea service, a tray of sandwiches and an oblong fruit cake.

'Now, Jason, would ye like me to tell ye all about this fine place ye've come to?' asks Uncle Charles.

'Yes, please!' Jason says eagerly.

As he eats heartily, he listens intently to Uncle who informs him of all the unusual landforms of the area. He begins to imagine a valley with no stream because it's hidden underground, and the cave where, deep inside, the water can be seen flowing by; but he pays most attention once the bays and seashore are mentioned.

In particular, he notes the description of the coastal path from Longbeach to Traxi Point and on to Blackledge, the local names for these land marks. Uncle emphasises that in places the path is precariously close to the cliff edge.

'Gracious, Jason, you are hungry; you seem to like the bara brith!' exclaims Aunty Gertie.

'It's all delicious,' he replies, 'such tasty ham, and yes, I love the fruit loaf.'

He continues listening to his uncle. Jason already knows that the coastline has very big tides and that vast expanses of rock and sand are uncovered when the sea recedes, but he has no idea of where to go looking for prawns except for the bay his father has spoken of— and that was a time-tinted memory of his outings during his own childhood when he lived in the village before moving to the Midlands at twenty, never to return.

Jason's attention is drawn many times to strict warnings about the dangers of the seas around the area. While he listens, he imagines many trips exploring the secret parts of the shores, but powerful descriptions of turbulent tides bring him back to reality, and he cannot dismiss thoughts of the sea's ruthless power that can catch out the unwary. The warning is clearly set in his mind and Aunty nods as she realises, he's taken it in.

'We are not exaggerating, darling, we have seen many tragedies on this coast,' she says, 'so, please heed all the advice. We know from Janet and Bob that you're an excellent swimmer, but even the strongest can't swim against the worst currents here.'

'Please don't worry, I promise I will be so careful,' he replies sincerely.

Jason unpacks his clothes and puts them meticulously onto the shelves in the small wardrobe and hangs up his Sunday suit neatly draped with his school tie. He reads a letter from his mother which instructs him how to behave at all times and not to miss church for his planned outdoor activities.

He looks at the new prawn net and wonders when he might have it full of jumping shellfish, for he has never seen a live prawn in his life. His mind drifts to the beach in his imagination and he sees the three large shallow pools described to him by his father, and he wonders if he will find them or if they are actually there at all.

Supper is beans on toast with grated cheese grilled to sizzling on top and enhanced with Worcester sauce, two additions to beans he's not tried before.

'Wow! This looks different!' Jason exclaims.

Aunty smiles.

'Simply the savoury sauce and the sweetness of the cheddar,' Uncle Charles cuts in, 'what you think, eh Jason? Good warming stuff!'

'It certainly beats plain beans on toast!' Jason laughs, as he cleans the plate neatly with his knife, carefully placing every last bean on the back of his fork. He sips a glass of orange squash, and has a thin slice of fruit cake to finish.

Without prompting, he stands to go upstairs to bed at eight O'clock. Looking a little apprehensive, he says, 'Goodnight, Aunty, Uncle, and thank you for making me so welcome. I can't wait to get to the beach tomorrow.'

'It's a pleasure, Jason. We know it's your first night away from home, but there's nothing to fear. Try to relax and sleep well!' Aunty clutches his arm on seeing it trembling slightly.

He smiles and heads for his room where he takes out his *Pocket Guide to the Seashore* and reads avidly for half an hour until he is fast asleep.

Early the following morning, he wakes and glances at his bedside clock. It is seven o'clock and he can see the sky is bright and blue with hazy sunshine already making a glow. The silvery sea is shimmering and he yearns to put his feet into the saline waves for the first time. He sneaks quietly downstairs and out into the garden.

Over supper, Uncle Charles outlined all the plants, vegetables and flowers that he grows and Jason is keen to see them. From a small concrete yard, he strides up three steps to the garden where a central path has rows of vegetables on one side and many daffodils, a few late crocuses, hyacinths and azaleas on the other. He takes a compass from his pocket and sees the area is south-facing, in fact southeast to northwest, so it will have the sun most of the day.

He examines the neat rows of root vegetables and slowly, the sun inches around the corner of the adjoining house bringing the first rays of warmth to the garden. There are many small birds darting amongst the flowers and fluttering in small flocks from the neighbouring properties as they go in pursuit of their daily feed of seeds and insects. He listens intently to the twittering birds, then the tranquillity is suddenly broken.

'Don't worry, Master Jason, I'll soon have ye' diggin' the garden for me, helping me spread the manure and hoeing the weeds, ha, ha, ha!' A friendly voice rings out as Uncle trudges up the steps to join him. 'Look, beetroot, swedes, parsnips; soon the spring cabbage will be ready. And over there,' he points to a sunny corner, 'the first asparagus is just comin' through. The potatoes, their mauve green shoots are just showin'; grown in seaweed, they're very special, ye'll taste them some time.'

Jason's eyes set on a small greenhouse propped against a white-washed wall. 'Tomatoes from that little thing keep Gertie and I going all summer, and a few cucumbers as well. There's plenty more too. We don't buy anything! Later, we'll have gooseberries then raspberries, see the tall canes, that's where.' He chuckles with his own self-satisfaction.

Jason looks on in awe, as it's all new for him. 'I can't believe how there is so much growing already. The allotments back home have very little but swedes and cabbages at the moment! Dad doesn't have time for gardening, so we have tinned vegetables mainly.'

'Ah, here it's much milder because of the Gulf Stream that brings warm water to our shores, so we don't have much frost. Further west they have no frost at all. But mind you, ten years ago we had the harshest winter in memory. It froze everything and killed many plants and birds particularly; I hope we never have that again,' Uncle says shaking his head.

'I was very young then and don't remember it. But this April, it's lovely and warm here, so I guess I am lucky!' Jason smiles.

Charles smiles too. 'But ye didn't come here to stay for the garden. Ye look excited, so what's your plan today?'

'I'd really like to go to the beach today. I want to catch some prawns, I hope...' Jason says.

'Aye, low tide will be early afternoon. Did ye see the moon last night? It's waxing, so in a few days, at the full moon, ye'll see a very low tide. I'll check the time in the paper...time and tide and all that, ye know.'

They sit on his considering bench—so named as it's where he sits every day for a while to plan his day and consider all the work that's needed.

'Now, to get to Longbeach; ye take the bus from the square or on the hill to the bay. Will cost a penny, but worth it as the hill is quite long and the pavement narrow, then it's a long windy way down to the bay. The pools Dad spoke of will uncover in the middle about an hour before low tide. Only go there as everyone can see ye clearly and don't venture further.'

Jason takes it all in, nodding several times.

'Ye have to understand the tides,' Uncle continues. 'Nearly forty foot today, even more by the weekend. The tide comes in in six hours, goes out in six hours. Set ye watch by it. Six into forty means nearly seven feet of flood tide every hour, enough to cover ye tallest man. Ye understand? See what I'm getting at? Ye don't take any risks. Always stay in sight of the shore, so don't go outside the bay and don't go far into the sea. It's still cold and ye currents are lethal, just like bullies!' He pauses for emphasis. 'They'll suck ye away with the strength of a serpent. Ye cannot swim against them. They'll swallow ye up! Well, I think that's enough lecturing for today!' He smiles, patting Jason's shoulder in assurance.

'Yes, Uncle,' he says obediently, 'I understand.'

'Good! We're very happy to have you coming and going as you please. We want you to have the most out of your stay here, and you're a level-headed lad; you'll be careful—just don't get carried away or lost, will you?'

'No, Uncle, I'll be sensible.'

At half past nine, having eaten cereal and toast for breakfast, he is at the door having donned the black plimsolls the gym master gave him. They are worn and tattered but perfect for the rough rocks and he has short white socks to protect his ankles. Uncle hands him a brown webbing bag with shoulder strap.

'My old gas mask haversack from the war, just the thing; and inside, there's a plastic bottle of squash and some food for ye.' Jason opens it and sees the thick plastic container, together with sandwiches wrapped in bread paper, and beams at the bar of chocolate which for him is a special treat. He kisses Aunty's cheek and shakes Uncle's hand, and with prawn net aloft, he sets off towards the bus stop, turning twice to wave as he trots happily along.

Watching him, Gertie sighs. 'He's a very young twelve-year-old, very slight and tender; and such spindly little legs, and his voice sounds as sweet as a linnet. I do hope you have set him right, Charles, because you know I won't relax till he's safely home. Maybe the brisk exercise on the rocks will build up his muscles and toughen him up a bit. Having him here is quite a responsibility.'

'Aye, after all, he is the son they thought would never happen. Janet always said she wanted a big family, but the war put paid to that. Poor Bob's injuries, though he recovered well over the years, were pretty severe. They said he'd never be a father, yet he proved them wrong eventually. So, Jason's been very cossetted.'

Gertie nods thoughtfully. 'I was a little surprised they agreed to him coming here; travelling on his own as well...so maybe I am a little anxious.' Then she smiles. 'But his enthusiasm is obvious.'

Jason walks briskly to the bus station. When the bus arrives, he steps on, parks his net under the stairs and goes to the top deck and to the front seats for the best view. As the bus motors up the winding road, a leafy branch beats against the front window making Jason jump up, but it is knocked aside. After one stop, the bus begins to descend slowly down a hill and now Jason can see the sea and the headland of the bay far to the west.

The second it pulls in on the slip road above the shore he leaps off and dashes down the concrete steps to the shingle. In four paces he is on the sand for the first time and he feels a wonderful sense of freedom. He sits on a dry patch and draws two armfuls of the golden grains to his side, rolling on it like a dog drying itself after a bath. Then he springs to his feet and trots down towards the sea. The dull and dreary days of school seem far away, and apart from a few sea gulls, he seems to have the place for himself.

He dances in joy, knowing, for once, nobody is watching him. How different it is from school where his every step in the playground and on the sports field is watched by critical eyes. He does not see the unfriendly faces that have bullied him so often. At last, he feels free.

The sand is wet and soggy and looking back, he can see his own footprints from his cavorting. The first boulders begin to show to his right as the gentle waves wash in continual rhythm and within minutes, as he stares in fascination, more and more rounded rocks emerge from the receding sea. A little way beyond, a patch of white-water forms as the tide breaks over a submerged reef. Many seagulls sit on the water between him and the headland as though patiently awaiting some edible treats.

Using the pole of his net for guidance, carefully he takes his first step into the sea. The cool swirling water is therapeutic and relaxing, easing his anxiety, and he wades a little further until knee deep. The gentle waves splash his shorts and he ventures until they are soaked at the rim. He looks at his pale legs and feels the rays of the sunshine intermittently drying the saline water. He stands and gazes out to sea, and as though a plug has been pulled, the tide continues to disappear rapidly.

Soon, the reef emerges from the white waves and he can make out a large enclosed area of still water which he believes could be one of the prawn pools he is looking for. He imagines his father in this very spot, waiting with anticipation of a catch all those years ago, just as he is doing now.

He makes every step carefully as the seaweed under his feet is wet and slippery. His eyes begin to focus on the myriad of different coloured sea plants, and on the small periwinkles and other creatures hiding within. He is pleased to identify several from his recent reading. He leaves his haversack on a flat rock close to the large pool and scrambles over the other rocks towards the reef. He slips and slides over the weed-strewn surfaces.

Suddenly, he loses his footing completely and tumbles into a shallow gully, soaking his shorts and the back of his tee shirt, but undeterred, he scrambles on and begins prodding under the overhanging weed with the handle of his net. Then, in a narrow fissure, he spots a small crab which, again, he recognises from his seashore guide, but it is lodged in the crack and difficult to reach.

Quickly, his young eyes become attuned to the formations of the limestone rocks, and he spots another crab and yet another, but they have all chosen their hiding places well, and he fails to dislodge any of them.

Then in a corner of a shallow pool, he can make out the oval outline of a much bigger crab. Its brown shell is unmistakable and the depth of water and reflections make it appear quite large. It is partly obscured by some flat brown weed described in his book as horsetail. He can see his net will be useless to dislodge the crab and, breathing deeply, he crouches down and gently slides his hand into the water towards the creature. But the pool is much deeper than it appears and he stoops till most of his shorts are in the water. Just as he reaches to touch it he disturbs something from under the weed that makes him start. He feels a sharp nip on his index finger then another on his thumb and something with two bright red eyes and flailing blue tipped claws slashes at his hand repeatedly.

With a startled cry, he jumps back, slipping on the smooth stones and ending up on his back, soaking all his clothes. He wriggles himself to his feet, his slipping and sliding causing the water to cloud to a gun-metal darkness. He gasps as his index finger oozes a thin stream of blood from the sharp angry nip. The rocks of the reef now seem more forbidding and he scrambles nervously across the boulders back to the safety of the flat rocks where he left his haversack. Close to crying, even though he tries to suppress his shock, he munches the bar of chocolate and has a good swig of orange squash.

He takes off his shirt and attempts to wring the water out then spreads it on the rocks, hoping it will partially dry in the warm sun. Feeling better, he takes his net and haversack and wades into the pool which is now no deeper than his knees. Many large flat stones are partly or fully submerged; he believes this could the right place to find prawns. Hastily, he plunges his net under some weed and as he scoops it out, he spots many little creatures darting away, but the net itself is empty.

In five scoops, he catches nothing yet he sees many more shapes that elude him. Then he works the net around the base of a large slab, pulling it through the seaweed that drapes into the darkness of the deeper water. His face lights up when he sees the net alive with a host of wriggling creatures amongst some green seaweed. Several large prawns are translucent green-brown in colour, with twitching legs, flapping tails, bulbous eyes and long antennae. He puts his hand into the net, but all elude him, jumping around as he attempts to clutch them in his quivering hand. In the net there's also a small rock fish and two scurrying small green crabs, and he is a tad wary of these as their claws, though small, could possibly inflict another nasty nip.

He grabs the largest prawn that's longer than his middle finger, but tail flapping, it wriggles too quickly for him, slips from his grasp and disappears into the pool below. The second he tries to grab by the antennae, but it too slips through his fingers and eludes the open bag. The third, he grasps firmly with his full open palm, clutching determinedly until he releases it into the bottom of his haversack. His first prawn! He beams in triumph then carries on scooping under the overhanging weed, hoping for more success.

Methodically, he covers most of the rocks in the sun- drenched pool, which he has now stirred up to a peaty green, yet he continues to be successful with almost every stroke of the net. He thinks how proud his father would be, as he has not only found the pools but has had a good catch on his very first prawning day.

So intense is his concentration, he does not realise that the sea is getting deeper around him. Suddenly, he looks up and it is about to swamp his shirt, the lunch pack and squash bottle he placed on the flat rock. In his haste to get them, he stumbles twice on submerged stones, yet he ensures the catch is held high above the water, even though he soaks himself. Shaking with excitement and triumph, he munches the ham sandwiches and swigs the orange squash, then he dons his damp shirt and starts to make his way back up the shore towards the bus stop.

He stares across the sand and notices that the field behind the sea wall, which was empty before, is now half full of large white single-decker buses. They have brought dozens of day trippers to the beach. Numerous rows and rings of deck chairs cover much of the upper beach away from the wetter sand. There is a drone of chatter from people that the gentle noise of the waves had suppressed. It is no longer the vacant and tranquil place he so valued. He realises that now he looks like a beach urchin in damp beach clothes, yet triumphant. Soon he reaches them. He paces past several groups and thinks they are laughing at him with his skinny pale legs.

'What ya catch, boy?' calls out a rough-looking man in his twenties. He is dressed in a check shirt with grey flannel trousers and a cloth cap perched at a cheeky angle on his head.

'Prawns!' Jason calls back and continues walking.

'Posh little *crwt*, hmmm…' he hears but does not flinch or look back. He doesn't know what *crwt* means, but doesn't like the sound of it.

'You mam will give you, getting home soaked and dirty!' A large lady shouts across a ring of deck chairs. 'You'll 'ave a wack *cythrul*,' she squawks. Despite his anxiety, Jason chuckles to himself, yet he almost bumps into the man in the cap.

'Show us your catch then,' he snarls at uneasy Jason.

'I have to catch that bus!' Jason points towards the land, trying to distract the man. Jason panics and scurries past him and runs across the soft sand as fast as he can until he reaches the shingle.

Soon, he is safely seated on the bus having places his wet net under the stairs. Relieved as it sets off up the hill, he smiles and relaxes and peeps into the haversack to admire his catch. At the same time, he feels a twinge of pain, and notices that his finger is still weeping a light trail of blood from the nip of the red-eyed crab. *What a day!* he thinks. *My first catch is worth a little pain. But I'll be more careful next time.*

Velvet swimming or fiddler crab

Chapter Two

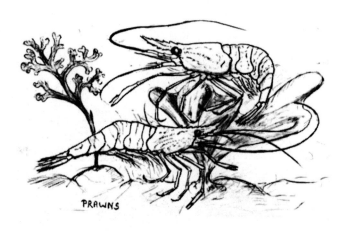

Prawns

Wise Advice

Late that afternoon, Jason stands next to Aunty Gertie in the scullery. Having had a long hot bath, he now feels refreshed. He has changed into crisp white shorts, a clean shirt and a comforting pullover.

His legs have many small scratches and scrapes from the jagged rocks and sharp barnacles, his index finger has a small cut and his thumb has a bruise by the nail from the nip of the crab. At Aunty Gertie's insistence, he has washed them carefully, and rubbed iodine on both.

Outside, his washed clothes flap gently on the line, while a pot of water simmers on the hob in the scullery. Aunty Gertie tosses in a spoonful of salt then takes the bowl with his catch of prawns, 'How clever of you to bring us these!' she says—and still jumping they are tipped mercilessly into the seething liquid.

Jason starts as his catch is swiftly killed then watches intently as the green-tinged opaque shells turn to a bright orange red in seconds. Gertie swirls the water as it begins to bubble then switches the gas off.

24

After a minute, she inverts the pan over a colander in the sink and drains away the water, tipping the steaming shellfish into a plastic bowl.

Uncle Charles walks in. 'Cor, lovely smell, I could get the waft from the garden! Try one hot from the pot; this is how they're best. Ye'll never taste better.' Deftly, he takes one, blowing on it to cool it down, then twists the body and the tail to pull the succulent meat out in one neat piece. 'Here, ye taste, first of ya catch!' He holds it out towards Jason who takes it with glee, popping the curled pink shellfish into his mouth in one.

'That's taste eh? Not had one so fresh in years.'

Jason nods. 'I've never had one before. It's wonderful.'

'Ye must go again!' says Charles with a laugh.

'Now, Charles, we should sit at the table to do Jason's catch justice,' says Gertie.

Very soon, they are sitting around the table, the bowl in the middle and a loaf of brown bread with a slab of butter on the side, and a pot of salad cream. Gertie quickly slices the bread and butters it.

'There, everything's ready,' she says. 'We may begin.'

Jason, between his effusive gorging asks, 'You like crab, Uncle? I must learn to catch those next! I saw some, one was quite big, but couldn't catch it. But I'll try again.'

'Ye bet! Crab is the tastiest meat from the sea. And everyone agrees that the crab from here, particularly a cow—that's the female—in the summer, is the finest of all on the coast. See, further round, there're lots of mussel beds—they never grow to size because of the rough autumn and winter seas, but crabs must feed on them and their taste ain't as good as here, where they feed on other small crustaceans and seaweed. Ye'll see. What ye need is a crab hook. We don't have one; loaned it out long ago, and like many things that go to the sea, it never came back,' Charles chortles and takes another prawn, peels and downs it in one.

'Where can I buy a hook… are they expensive?' Jason asks nervously.

Gertie comes in having topped up the tea pot. 'Darling, go and see Mr Windston, the blacksmith, down the lane behind the village hall. He will make you one for a couple of shillings. I'll give you half a crown; that should cover it. Take it as a little present for you.'

'Thank you, Aunty! I'll pay you back with lots of crabs and more prawns. Will he be open early? It would be good to have one for the tide tomorrow!' Jason enthuses.

Gertie laughs. 'He will be there before you're up I'm quite sure. Just ask the lovely people in the paper shop opposite the end of this road— the gentle-looking man with a small grey beard is called Mr David—if you're not sure of the way. Then it's only a few hundred yards away,' she assures as they continue peeling and savouring the prawns with the brown bread and butter and salad cream.

'Well, Jason, you have done us proud today. I remember your father bringing them home on the odd occasion, and that was long, long ago!' Charles says.

'And as fresh as this, it is such a treat!' Gertie adds.

Jason beams. 'Well, I must be up early to go to the blacksmith. I hope he can make me a hook for tomorrow, as after tasting these prawns, I can't wait to try crab. So, I must go to bed now. Thank you, Aunty, Uncle. It's been a wonderful start to my holiday.'

Jason's anticipation takes him into dreams of the seashore and the numerous places to explore, where, most of all, he can enjoy his own freedom away from the boys in school. His fantasies now focus on the wild and rugged rocks of the low tide and what he might find in the pools and crevices. Usually, his dreams drift into nightmares fuelled by his bad experiences with several boys at school. When he sees a dark corner on the rocks in the voyages in his dreams, lurking somewhere there are the sour faces of those he wants to forget.

Very early on Thursday morning, he goes down stairs. In front of the aged cast iron, tarnished-cream cooking range, his dry clothes hang neatly on a wooden frame. They feel comforting and warm as he slips them on, gripping him snugly as he laces up his shoes. He trots over to the paper shop where Mr David gives him directions to the blacksmith. He leads Jason to the door and points the way precisely.

At that moment, an old man, wizened and stooped with drooping shoulders and a wrinkled weather-beaten face topped by wispy white hair, shuffles down the pavement. He uses two walking sticks and sits on the end of the low wall that separates the adjacent property from the shop.

'Morning, Joe. This boy wants a crab hook. Will you take him on the rocks?' Mr David calls to the old man in a raised voice. Jason thinks the man is far too old to go to the rocks. The old man looks up, shakes his head, then beckons to Jason come and to talk to him. Nervously, he goes across and stops a few paces away.

'Hello, Sir,' he says politely in his clear young voice. 'It's my first time here. I'm staying with my relations, Charles and Gertie Clark. I want to go crabbing today and I'm hoping Mr Windston, the blacksmith, will make me a crabbing hook, today if possible. I want to go down to the rocks at Longbeach in time for the low tide.'

'Aye, it's a low tide, cos the moon's a waxing,' Joe says in a slightly halting tone. 'Aye, will be full moon in two days, lowest tide in four, so you've good days of scouring ahead. Ha, ha, but *where* to scour is the mystery. Wish I could get there myself,' he sighs and gazes in the direction of the sea through the slits of his watery blue eyes.

'I saw come crabs yesterday, that's why I need a hook to get them out,' Jason explains.

'Windston will make t h e hook. But listen, boy, must be three feet long of round mild steel, a quarter of an inch in diameter. Five-eighths if he has it is better, stronger. It must be filed to a point either end. It must be bent one end at right angles to fit into pole, the other end bent opposite way rounded to shape of thumb. Huh, how big's your thumb?' Joe says holding up his withered right hand with its short, stumpy, bent fingers and thick, sturdy thumb.

'Gottit, boy! Get a hoe handle four feet long. Williams the hardware shop has these. Find him down the hill to right. Windston'll be in the workshop for sure. Tell him Old Joe sent ye, so do a good job of it.' Short of breath, Joe gazes at the sky blankly, even though his mind is still working. 'Best place for crabs is the Blackledge; half mile round ye Traxi Point,' he continues. 'Ye'll see ye old wreck, stern of a big iron ship sticking out yonder. Keep from there. Take coastal path from the bay to four old iron pillars, remains of a windmill. There, and only there— nowhere else—is an easy path down to rocks. But watch tide, floods ever so quickly. Aye, aye...'

27

Jason sees that the energy has now gone from Joe, and he is anxious not to exhaust the old man. 'Thank you, Mr Joe, thank you. I must hurry now, and I really hope Mr Windston can make it today. See you later, Sir.' He moves off, waves and then hurries around the corner to look for the blacksmith.

Following Mr David's directions, he walks along a narrow lane with a bramble-ravaged hedge on one side, and immediately, he can hear the banging of metal. He approaches the rickety door of the low dark building which is set alongside a newer part with two storeys. The battered, brown entrance door is open at the top, above a solidly shut lower part.

On tiptoe, he manages to see over the half door. Flashes of silver and cobalt blue ignite the dingy darkness every few seconds, followed by the loud metallic bangs and crashes of a heavy hammer. Far in the depth of the building, he can just make out a stocky man bent over a workbench, illuminated by the regular flashes of light that make Jason jump every time. Jason stretches up and presses a round tarnished button and can just make out a feeble ring that's drowned by the almost continual clatter.

He waits several minutes then tries again, then a third and a fourth time, but all to no avail. He does not dare to venture inside and keeps his hand poised until there is a tiny lapse in the din. It rings for many seconds, then there is another enormous bang and a flash of blue lights and fiery orange sparks giving a moment of brightness, so he can for a split second see the man look up towards him. Three more loud bangs make him leap again and a deep voice utters something he cannot make out. Then from the depths, clad in dark oily clothes topped by a rounded black helmet with a curved shiny front that's thick with black soot, the man starts to move towards him.

Thinking of a creature from a space story, Jason trembles as he approaches, then the man lifts the front of the helmet to show his leathery face tarnished with days of grime. The large bloodshot eyes seem to stare at Jason menacingly.

'Mr Windston, can you please make me a crab hook?' he says hesitantly. 'Mr Joe sent me!'

The name causes the man to take note, and he smiles. 'I'll 'ave five minutes later on today. Know what Joe wants. Three feet mild steel bent both ways, an all that...'

'But I'm hoping to go down for the low tide today; it's just after midday, and I don't have a hook,' Jason says pleadingly.

The man's face softens as he can see his own two boys when they were that age and he smiles again. 'First big tides this year, shame to miss them. Go along and get a pole from Williams while I bend the iron. Then I will fix it to the wood for ye, and the first crab is mine. Be one shilling and nine pence. Pay me tomorrow if y'want. Now, go to get the hoe handle, four feet.'

Jason beams and runs along the lane nearly bumping into two ladies as he bustles around a corner. He runs down to the hardware shop, where in a tall pot in a corner is an assortment of garden tool handles. He purchases one four foot in length for six pence, and runs back to the blacksmith's workshop, hardly stopping for breath.

In little over an hour, at ten fifteen, he is back at his Uncle's holding his new crab hook. It is six foot six in length and towers over him, but he holds it by the end of the wood comfortably and proudly. He is anxious to set off for the beach to be in plenty of time for the low tide. The table is set for breakfast, but Uncle Charles and Aunty Gertie can both see his excitement and let him eat his breakfast in haste. Quickly, he downs a bowl of shredded wheat that is now soggy from soaking in milk for over an hour, followed by two cold pieces of toast spread with the delicious orange marmalade Aunty made earlier in the year.

'I know how excited you are, but clean your teeth before you go, Jason,' says Gertie with a laugh.

'Oh, yes!' says Jason, and he rushes upstairs. As soon as he can, he grabs his haversack that Gertie has already loaded with his picnic. She has also packed, neatly in a brown paper bag, a spare pair of shorts should he get wet again.

'Off you go!' she says at the door, and ruffles his hair. Soon, he is bouncing to the bus stop, smiling broadly all the way.

He waits at the first stop from the bus station and stares anxiously down the road, but there is no sign of a bus. After nearly fifteen minutes of increasing anxiety, he sees the bus crawl its way up the small incline to the stop. Six or more people queuing push their way on as soon as three passengers get off. Politely, Jason allows them to pass then steps onto the platform to see a stocky officious-looking conductor with a bulging red face confronting him.

'Can't bring that aboard, it will poke an eye out. Off!'

'It'll go under the stairs...' Jason pleads.

'No! It's too long. Off, off!'

The conductor rings the bell and the bus pulls away, leaving Jason standing alone on the pavement, and he almost bursts into tears.

'Bully!' he shouts, repeating it many times. Wiping his blushing face, he starts to walk the long road to the beach, following the bus route. He is anxious, knowing there isn't that much time before the low tide, after which the sea will start to flood again. He strides with all his energy, not stopping to take breath at all. The narrow pavement is unfriendly as cars and other vehicles pass at speed and he can hardly hold back his tears and his anger.

When he passes the brow of the hill and starts the descent to the beach, his spirit rises as the sea comes into sight. Still, it has taken nearly half an hour to get to the steps down to the shingle shoreline. He guesses the tide is not far from the turn, but it is out much further than on the previous day, and has uncovered hundreds of yards of rocks to explore.

He heads for the reef imagining the bounty of crabs hidden away; then he sees the outline of a male figure climbing from a gully carrying a sack over his shoulder. He appears to be searching the area methodically. Jason's high hopes are now dashed and he stands and stares, just managing to maintain his composure.

Perhaps, I should go to Blackledge as Joe suggested, he thinks, yet he knows he is not allowed to go around the point alone. He takes the rough map he has sketched out from the haversack and decides he will go to look there anyway. He scrambles across the rocks to the base of the cliff where he can see a rough but manageable track up the steeper rocks that leads to the main cliff path above.

The rocky track seems never-ending as he ascends the gentle slope, but when he stops and looks back, it seems far steeper than it appeared. Then as he clambers further, it becomes more difficult, and he has to grip the rocks firmly with both his hands, at the same time finding secure footings below him. It is not the easy climb it appeared to be from below.

Eventually, he reaches the summit and heaves his trembling body onto the safety of the compacted soil path. He thinks back to the simple rock climbing he has done with his father, and feels grateful for all the wise precautions that have been drummed into him.

He sits panting and gazes back over the shore awhile, with an eye still on the figure on the reef. Then briskly, he picks himself up and marches along the path perched high above the exposed rocks. In places the path narrows, becoming uneven, rough and muddy, with some parts precariously near to precipitous drops to the rocks below. In the distance, he can see Blackledge, a distinctive shelf of rocks with small waves breaking over the shape of the wreck a short way out to sea. Close to it, several clusters of wave-rounded weed-strewn boulders wash gently in the waves.

The path twists around the cliff, traversing little coves and deep gullies. Now he is much closer to his destination and he looks down and sees the shelving strata that give Blackledge its name. Somewhat exhausted and anxious, he rounds a corner to find the iron pillars and the junction with the well-trodden track that leads down to the rocks below, exactly as Joe described.

It's a relief when, finally, Jason feels the cool of the sea as he plunges knee-deep into the first sandy pool he sees. Yet, he notices that many of the boulders by the wreck have now disappeared, and the tide is obviously flooding. He follows a narrow gully towards the sea, diligently looking in every crevice in the hope of finding a sizeable crab, but all he sees are very small ones wedged in tiny fissures, and so he hastens on. He disturbs a herring gull that squawks angrily as it takes off, leaving behind a large soft shell of a crab pecked into pieces. He flicks away the overhanging seaweed with his hook and searches every crack in the rocks, but does not see a single large crab similar to the one he tried in vain to catch on his first outing. Somewhat dejected after twenty minutes of searching, he heads back towards the rock face and to the track that will lead him homewards.

Close to the base of the cliff, he crosses a broken patch of rock that has some tall upright stones in formations which could make a small but challenging rock climb. One upright rock has many cracks parallel to the ground that make easy foot holes, so he decides to climb the few feet to the top. Just as he is about to put the tip of his plimsoll into the lowest crack, he bends down to check that no fiddler crabs are lurking inside. Suddenly, his face lights up as he spots, wedged in the darkness of the depths of the fissure, an oval shell far larger than anything he has seen.

He puts his haversack safely on an adjacent rock then squats down and gingerly slides the hook towards the side of the shell where a big claw is neatly tucked underneath. He is aiming to get the hook behind the crab—just as Joe had told him to do. The split second he touches the shell the creature flinches, arching itself firmly into a corner from where it does not intend to move. Whatever angle Jason tries, he cannot dislodge the crab, and the obstinate creature wedges itself more firmly into the narrow crack in the rock.

The sea is approaching rapidly and now washes around his feet, as a larger wave splashes over the crab. In one last desperate try, he wriggles the hook under the shell between the legs of the crab and suddenly, he feels it give a tiny amount. Trembling, he keeps the hook under the crab, jerking it gently to induce some movement. The crab gives a fraction again, and slowly, it inches towards him as he gradually withdraws the iron hook. Then it firmly clasps the metal with one claw, and Jason pulls it slowly towards him, eventually easing it clear of the cleft in the rock.

At that second, another wave pounds the rock and the crab releases its grip on the hook and it drops away into the foaming waves and disappears, much to Jason's despair. As the water recedes momentarily, he spots the rounded shell with large claws splayed either side as it scurries away. Instinctively, he drops the hook and with both palms open plunges through the frothy white water towards his prize. He lands on it firmly but feels the creature struggling to escape. He keeps his hands firmly pressing down while more waves splash around him, soaking him to the waist. He doesn't notice that his knee is bleeding from crashing against a sharp barnacle-covered boulder and he wriggles to his feet, clasping his first crab triumphantly in both hands.

He stands tall in the frothy water, then anchors the crab onto a rock with one hand and pulls a clump of wrack from a boulder with the other. He turns the crab over and it immediately clasps onto the weed. Shaking with excitement, he plunges the creature into his haversack and fastens the buckle securely. He slings his haversack over his shoulder, then retrieves his hook and net and wades through the advancing water to the base of the cliff.

Safely away from the flooding tide, he changes into dry shorts then sits and munches his sandwiches. He keeps peering into his haversack on the rock beside him, repeating out loud to the seagulls, 'I've caught a crab, I've caught a crab, well done, sir, well done, sir!' and smiles to himself in triumph. He then picks up his gear and sets off to ascend to the steep path that will eventually take him home. Such is his elation, he scrambles up the track to the cliff path without stopping or glancing either way. As he walks briskly along the lofty cliff path, he totally ignores several rough-looking day trippers who pass him and soon he is back on Longbeach.

Emboldened by his achievement, he decides to take a winding set of steps beyond the bus stop that lead through a dark wood to the brow of the hill, one of the local paths Uncle Charles had outlined to him. He remembers its name—Parson's Wood—and this route cuts off the long corner in the road. But half way up the long flight of steps, he sees ahead of him four burly teenage boys shouting at each other and laughing coarsely. They are making gestures to one another as they approach Jason.

One glares directly at him and he fears a confrontation and hesitates. Then his newly-found pride and confidence surges and he strides up the steps undaunted. They are so absorbed in banter that he manages to go past them and continue without a word exchanged, but the dark look from one is set in his mind.

He continues in a confident pace, flexing his body, and proud of himself for once not being a coward. Totally excited, he arrives at his holiday home shortly after three thirty.

'Look at this!' he says as soon as he is through the door.

Uncle Charles examines the fine crab, 'Well done! It certainly looks big enough,' and he takes a ruler to measure its size and nods in approval. 'It's five and a quarter inches, well over ye legal size of four and a half. What a good catch, bravo! And see ye here, it's a bull crab, look at the narrow tail and big claws. A cow is the opposite, wide tail and smaller claws. Hope Gertie remembers to buy the salad cream as we ate it all with the prawns last night. This will be a real treat.'

He puts a saucepan of water on the range while Jason goes up for a bath, as he got totally drenched again when he caught the crab. When he comes down after a very quick soak, he sneaks out, hoping to find old Joe by the paper shop opposite the end of the street. As earlier, he is sitting on the wall, his two sticks propped aside him.

'Hello, Mr Joe,' he calls, 'It's Jason.' He can contain his excitement no longer. 'Caught a crab today, with my new hook!'

'Aye, aye, boy. Ye sure 'tis big enough?' comes the gravelly response.

'It's five and a quarter inches—'

'Bull or cow?' Joe interrupts.

'A bull,' Jason says, remembering what Uncle Charles has told him.

'Huh! Cow's better. The back meat is sweeter. Never mind, next time. And when ye'll catch lots, can ye bring me a small cow for me supper. I would love to taste it again afore the old ship sinks.'

'Of course, I will, Mr Joe. I'll be trying again tomorrow. Bye, Mr Joe!'

'No, just a few minutes, ya listen t'me. I can see those rocks as clearly as the last day was there, many years ago. They don't change, nor ye crab holes and lobster pools. Been there forever. When ya walk down gully from base of rock...'

At this point, Jason has his sketchbook and pencil poised to make notes. For nearly ten minutes, he scribbles away, sketching the rocks exactly as Joe describes. Apart from the occasional "yes, yes" he says nothing but listens to the fascinating and detailed descriptions of the rocks and where he can find the best crab holes.

Suddenly, Joe tires visibly. 'That'll do ye for today. Remember a nice crab for Old Joe, please.'

'Yes, certainly sir,' Jason says with the greatest enthusiasm and gratitude and he leaps down the road like a young gazelle back to his uncle's house, where he writes up a journal of what he has done today. Then he hears Aunty Gertie's voice on returning from the shop where she works some afternoons and he heads downstairs.

'What a lovely crab, darling! You must be pleased. Your first, and with your new hook!' she smiles lovingly at Jason.

'I've cooked it so we can taste it this evening,' Charles says.

'We can have it before the kedgeree I've made for supper,' Gertie adds. 'I'll show you how to dress it, Jason. Do you want to watch me?'

'Yes, I certainly do!' he beams, and follows Gertie into the scullery.

The crab is on a plate on a small table next to the cooker.

Jason is taken back when he sees it, for both claws and some legs are separate from the rest of the crab, so it doesn't look quite as impressive. Gertie can see a look of disappointment on Jason's face as he picks up the clawless body.

'Darling, it's nothing Uncle Charles has done when cooking it. When they are cooked, exactly as I did the prawns, they usually shed some of their limbs, it's inevitable. It doesn't alter the taste, though. Now let me show you how to prepare it.'

Gertie puts on an apron and washes her hands while Jason watches intently as she dismembers the crab. In just ten minutes, she has a small bowl full of white meat on one side, and brown on the other. She passes Jason a small taster of each.

'Gosh, the brown meat is very strong,' he says taking a tiny morsel. Then he tries the white meat. 'That's delicious and sweet, but the brown meat certainly is very strong.' Then Gertie covers the bowl and puts it on the side.

'Now, Jason, have you written a letter to Mum and Dad? I have bought a post card so you can send that as well. Uncle has some stamps. Come down for supper in half an hour, please.'

When his tasks are done, Jason descends and goes into the small dining room. He sits at the table. On it is a bowl of salad cream, a vinegar shaker and a large plate of buttered brown bread. Charles has been listening to his favourite radio programme and enters the room chuckling to himself. He sits down alongside Jason and Aunty comes in with the bowl of crabmeat and places it in the middle of the table.

'Now, Jason, help yourself to the white meat and try a little of the brown as well,' Gertie says, then is interrupted by Charles.

'I'll show Jason how to make a dressed crab; it gets the best flavour from both the white and brown meat.'

'The brown is very strong. How is that when the white meat is so sweet?' Jason enquires.

'The white meat is always sweet. But brown meat from a bull can be strong; from the cow, dark meat is milder and sweeter.' Charles raises a finger. 'If ye catch a nice cow, ye'll see. That's a challenge!'

Gertie takes a modest amount of the white meat, leaving the rest for Charles.

'Watch this!' he says. 'A full teaspoon of salad cream, a good shake of vinegar and plenty of pepper, then mix all together, brown and white.'

He takes a fork and gently mixes the crabmeat in the bowl together with his additions. 'Try this!' he says, proffering a small amount to Jason. 'But it'll be better with a cow's dark meat—milder flavour—if ye manage to catch one!'

'Mmmm…it's nicer but I think I prefer the white meat alone. But I hope I catch some more so we can try a cow crab. Joe also says they're better, sweeter.'

They eat the crab piled onto buttered bread, clearing every scrap. Then Jason asks, 'What is kedgeree, Aunty?'

'It's made from smoked haddock, rice, vegetables and eggs. And I do a special sauce to go with it, curry sauce.' She smiles and clears the table shortly to return with a large bowl of steaming rice and a sauce boat. She serves a generous plateful to each.

'I've only had rice in a pudding, often on a Sunday. Dad loves it, particularly the brown skin. I've never had rice like this before. It's spicy and quite hot, isn't it?' Jason says, looking a little confused.

Uncle nudges him for assurance. 'Try mixing the sauce into the rice. That's how I like it.' He watches Jason take several mouthfuls and sees his expression of approval.

'The sea air gives a hearty appetite, doesn't it, Jason?' Aunty asks, as the three plates and serving bowl are left empty.

'It certainly does!' he says.

'Now, remember, see if ye can bring back a cow crab next time!' Charles says as Jason stands up to take himself to bed.

'I will. I have promised one to Mr Joe as well.'

'Hey, me first!' Uncle cuts in.

'Yes, of course,' Jason corrects himself, 'but he has told me of lots of places where I should look for crabs. He can describe the rocks exactly from his memory, so I hope tomorrow I will have lots of time to search for his secret places that he has shared with me.'

'He's obviously taken to you! He can be very gruff with lots of people, so you are very lucky,' Charles nods. 'Off ye go to bed then, and sweet dreams!'

'Good night, darling. I think you will sleep well tonight!' Gertie smiles.

Serrated or Toothed Wrack

Chapter Three

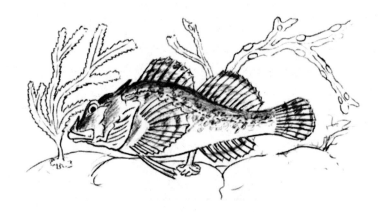

Bullhead or Bull Rout

Calm and Rough

'Today, I'm working at the bus and tram station,' says Uncle Charles over breakfast. 'They give me a few days most weeks, always a Friday, as since 'e railway finished here, there was no work for me on that line anymore.'

Jason nods, as he was puzzled why Uncle Charles didn't work every day.

'When the train came here,' Uncle Charles continues, 'anyone could get all over the country, and people from all over could get here. Now, they come from the hills in those common coaches, and only common people most of them. When I travelled as an inspector, we went to ye great cities, towns, resorts and spas throughout the land. The First Class always had many ladies and gentlemen travelling ye country. Aye, met some interesting people over the years.'

'It must have been wonderful being paid to go on a train every day, and going somewhere different. Almost like a mystery tour, Uncle,' Jason says with enthusiasm. 'Better than Dad who goes into the tin-plate works every day. He's always covered in dust from the machines when he gets home,' he sighs.

'Well, as a foreman and manager, your dad earns good money. The factory workers don't have it so good. It's hot and dangerous—not for Charles,' Gertie says.

'No, I chose a quieter life here. Don't earn your dad's money, but where'd ye rather be?' Charles says knowingly.

Jason smiles. 'I'll walk to the bus station with you, Uncle, if that's all right.'

They reach it in seven minutes. As they arrive, Uncle Charles looks at his watch. 'I'm early, so I can walk to the sea wall with you,' he says.

'That's wonderful!' Jason says.

'Let's see how much ye've learned. How many of ye birds can ye name, a few different ones already, perhaps?'

Jason shakes his head.

'Now, lad, there are three different gulls alone: a herring gull with grey wings, and a greater black back with dark slate wings. They're the bullies, particularly the black back.' Suddenly, he points something out, 'See ye one with a black head?'

'A black-headed gull?' Jason says tentatively.

'Right!' says Uncle, smiling. 'Lovely little birds. Only males have ye black head, and only in ye breeding season. After that, they have ye black spot behind the eye. Now they nest on the estuary twenty miles north from here. Other gulls nest on high cliffs. But eggs of black-headed are the most delicious of all. Perhaps ye'll taste one if I can get some.'

Jason looks astonished. 'Poor things! Raiding nests for food, it's cruel, isn't it?'

'Ah, well, it's an important story here. Ye see, they often nest too early and their eggs can be washed away on a flood or spring tide. If they have started incubation, it means no young are produced that season. Gathering the eggs makes them continue laying for several weeks, for until they have laid three eggs, called the clutch, they will not start incubating the eggs. Y' know, all birds sit on their eggs to keep them warm so the chicks develop in the egg. By delaying this until the end of April, when gathering gulls' eggs traditionally finishes, the worst of the wet weather and big spring tides have finished, so it's a much safer time to incubate. Also, when the young hatch in early June, there is far more feed about for the chicks, and the chances of their survival are much better. It's what's known as a symbiotic relationship between these gulls and humans...ah look, me bus is here, I must go. I'll tell ye more later. Meantime, see if ye can spot sanderlings, red shank, oyster catchers, and perhaps a curlew. See ye later, lad.' And Uncle trots across to the bus.

Jason stands on the sea wall looking down and notes how high the tide had come that morning. It's eight thirty and it has been ebbing for over an hour, and his heart is beating with excitement to get onto the rocks early for the best possible chance of a catch; some crabs and possibly prawns as well. He sets off to walk back home to prepare for his day. He knows Aunty will be there doing her daily chores.

The village is quiet with the first shops just beginning to open to empty streets. Jason walks up the hill looking in several windows. Williams, the ironmonger, has a row of flowering pot-plants outside. There's a lovely aroma coming from the bread shop for it has a small bakery behind. Every morning, the street has the waft of fresh baking bread.

Looking at the shops on the other side of the road, Jason observes how each building has individuality, even though they are all joined into one. They are all three-storey but the ironmonger has familiar sash windows, whereas the two upper floors of the bakery have taller windows that open in the centre. The largest of the shops, a rather posh men's outfitters, has bay windows on each floor with a curious central window that extends in one to all the levels, finishing with an elegant round top that nestles into the tiled roof. He knows he has seen this style of building before and stares up trying to think where.

Suddenly, Jason can hear a strange noise. It is a short repetitive sound in an odd rhythm—rather like the chants at a football match, he thinks. As he begins to ascend the hill, he can just make out Joe sitting, as usual, on the end of his wall. The din gets louder and a tall thick-set boy rushes towards Joe, followed by another and then they go out of sight. Jason walks briskly up the hill and can now make out words as he gets closer, but then he is hesitant and wary, sensing some unruliness. The queasy feeling he knows from school starts to build.

'Poor Old Joe!' he hears.

The boys in their late teens and early twenties are taunting the old man. Several older boys run towards Joe then veer away just before they reach him.

The jeering continues: 'Deaf Old Joe, blind Old Joe, poor Old Joe!' It's repeated several times, then there's a pause, then it continues after a few seconds. 'Mad Old Joe, deaf Old Joe, despised Old Joe, dying Old Joe!' As each boy rushes at Joe, he shouts the words directly into the old man's face.

Joe is waving a walking stick around his head in a useless attempt to hit one of them. Then he musters what's left of his long-spent strength and heaves himself to his feet, taking a few staggers forward, assisted by his two sticks.

'Any one of ya come 'ere!' he growls, spitting phlegm at the same time. There's a roar of derision from the boys and the chant starts up again.

'Mad Old Joe, deaf Old Joe, despised Old Joe, dying Old Joe!' The chants drone on and on.

Joe swings himself around on his stick and again issues a challenge. 'Any three of ya lily-liveried lot, come here!' he growls hopelessly into the air.

Once more, there is a peal of laughter and one boy stands behind Joe, who raises one stick in defiance as he tries to focus his faded blue eyes. Another boy calls to Joe from the side. He snarls and glares feebly at them. At that second, the boy behind kicks Joe's stick, unsteadying the old man who staggers and tumbles to the floor. Then three more dance over to him, and he lies there, helpless. They spit towards his face and then they all run away, repeating their ditty as they go: 'Poor Old Joe, blind Old Joe, dying Old Joe!' All the while as the frail old man tries to pull himself to his feet.

Jason is almost crying as he watches Joe in trouble, but knows he is incapable of aiding him. The louts have now run away, but then he notices that one boy with blonde hair is still standing a little distance away, his hands over his face as though ashamed. He looks at Joe, then Jason, and shakes his head. Then he hears the group calling to him, but he walks away not wishing to re-join them.

Jason calls, 'Joe, Joe, are you hurt, are you all right?' but his voice is too distressed and feeble for Joe to hear. As he approaches, he can hear Joe ranting.

The old man bellows, 'Nasty boys, 'orrid boys, boys is 'orrid, boys is 'orrid! Bully boys!' Now on his knees, he begins swinging a walking stick around his head again.

Jason shouts, 'Joe it's me, it's me, Jason. Those horrid boys, I'm so sorry, Joe.' But Joe is too mad to listen. 'It's me,' he repeats as he gets nearer to Joe.

''Orrid bully boys! Joe shouts again, not caring who hears as the message is for all.

Jason steps closer to him and Joe, brandishing his stick, begins slashing the air furiously. He catches Jason with a full blow to the upper arm. Jason screams and jumps back before another blow strikes. In great pain and shock, he holds his arm and begins to sob as he moves further away from the raging old man.

'Got ya, ya 'orrid bully boy!' he growls, although he cannot see who or where his victim is, and Jason runs the seventy yards down the road, pushes the front door open and scampers up to his room, where he collapses on his bed in tears.

As he sobs into his pillow, his hand caressing the bruised arm, he sees the faces of the boys spitting at Joe and his frail attempts to fight back. He knows he is the one who has taken the punishment for their callous cruelty and although it might have lifted Joe's ego, it certainly has deflated his.

He keeps repeating, 'Horrid bullies! Horrid bullies!' until his tears stop and his mind starts to drift to the ebbing tide and the wonderful earlier conversation with Joe, when he shared some of his secrets on where to find the best crab holes.

Feeling a little better, he hopes he can now see the rocks as vividly as they are in Joe's memory, firmly imprinted on his brain from having spent a lifetime scouring the rocks for all sorts of edible treasures.

Within thirty minutes, Jason is full of new enthusiasm. His Aunty did not hear him come in as she was in the greenhouse picking some lettuce for his sandwiches. This day, he has fresh prawns from his earlier success. Aunty has peeled and chopped them into some salad cream with a touch of pepper and vinegar. With shredded garden lettuce, these will make a delicious sandwich for his lunch on the rocks.

He does not bother to try the bus for fear of being turned off again. But when turning into the main road to follow the bus route, he notices there is no sign of Joe. He stops and ponders a few seconds, wondering what he could have done to help him. Perhaps he should have shouted at the ruffians to raise the alarm. He could have done something, but inside he has a great fear buried and he doesn't want to raise it. He feels the warmth of the sun on his face that lifts his spirits and he strides along the pavement at a brisk pace.

He follows the bus route until the road starts to descend and at this point, he turns right down the unmade road that leads to the short cut through Parson's Wood to the steps—the route he followed home the previous day. All the way, he wonders rather nervously if he will encounter anyone else this time.

When he arrives at the sea wall, he can see the tide is just half ebbed, yet there are some clouds beginning to build on the western skyline over the hills. His feet now almost follow a set pattern as he walks briskly around the cliff path and every time he rounds the corner of an inlet, his heart surges in expectation.

He takes great care clambering down the path that leads down to the Blackledge, then perches himself on a prominent rock so he can admire the scene as the tide rapidly recedes. He can see no one and delights in his solitude. Gentle waves swash over the wreck that seems far off shore. He sits and waits, staring as the shelving rocks emerge from the lapping seas. He feels well-prepared as he has memorised the notes that he carefully made as Joe described the layout and formations of the rocks.

Not wishing to get soaked yet again, he strips to his school swimming trunks and plimsolls and he is fully prepared for action. He folds his clothes and puts them, with his lunch pack, out of sight in a recess close to the entrance of a small tidal cave. With his empty haversack on his shoulder, he sets off to find Joe's secret locations.

The first place is on the side of a small standing rock in the corner of the eastern gully. He sees a promising crab in a round watery hole, and after a tussle for several minutes, it is his. He measures it on the gauge he has cut into the pole of the hook, following Joe's instructions. Unfortunately, it is just undersize and so is dropped into a deep pool for safety from other crabbers who might not be so scrupulous about the size limit. He counts the undersize crabs that marginally fail to be the size to keep and throws eight in all into the safety of deep pools.

He sees the tide is now well out. Following Joe's directions, he heads towards the wreck, then along a narrow gully. This conceals him from any other possible crabbers, but so far today, he thinks he is on the rocks of Blackledge alone. He spots the shallow pool Joe spoke of and underneath some dangling weed, he can see the round entrance of the special hole. He crouches down and soon sees a magnificent crab sideways on to him about two feet back in the hole.

He does not take his eye off the specimen as he slides his hook behind and over the carapace. Then gently, he starts to ease it forward on the slimy mud underneath. Suddenly, the crab splays both claws and arches upwards and the hook loses its anchor. The crab moves backwards and sideways and Jason begins to sense it could scurry out of sight into the unknown depths of the tunnel. He rakes at the crab frantically, each time failing to find a firm point.

Frustrated, he turns the hook over and attacks from the underneath. One great claw grips the steel firmly and in a series of gentle jerks, he eases the creature towards him gradually until the large brown-shelled crab is pulled from the dark. It drops into the shallow pool and immediately crawls away from him at remarkable speed. Jason plunges at the great carapace with both hands, pinning the flailing creature to the slippery round submerged rocks. Then relieved, and in triumph, he lifts his prize high above his head.

He is about to shout with joy, but suddenly, he is aware he is not alone as the sun has cast a person's shadow over the shallow pool. There is a clatter of clapping and a young girl who has been watching for several minutes shows her admiration.

'What a beauty, bravo!' the girl shouts.

Jason smiles a little. 'Who are you? Where did you come from, I didn't see you.'

The girl, in her early teens, is dressed in blue shorts and a white tee shirt and wears a pair of tennis shoes. She has short blonde hair and a well-tanned, smooth-skinned face dominated by striking blue eyes.

'Having a walk. Saw you and came to see what you're about. That crab's a beauty. Had any more?' she fires in a heavy accent. 'What's your name?'

'Jason, what's yours?' he says, putting a clump of seaweed onto the crab and pushing it into the haversack.

'Abby... rhymes with yabbie, big prawn-type creatures we catch back home. Do these crabs here taste any good?'

'Oh, yes, they do! But please don't tell anyone about this. Where I find them is a big secret,' he says, suddenly worried.

'How do you know the secrets? We all know fishermen are cagey about their secret places, cos they learn them from others of experience. Secrets, huh!' she replies in her clipped accent that's still puzzling Jason.

'Where are you from?' he asks politely.

'Isn't it obvious, or not met anyone from Australia before?'

'Not really—well, no, to be honest, but your tanned skin says something?' he says, glancing at his pale arms. 'Come on, I'll show you a few more secrets, but keep it quiet, won't you?'

'Don't worry, be an hanner to be with you, Jason. What other secrets do you have?' Abby jests. Then her smile fades a little. 'How did you get that big bruise on the arm?' She looks at him, senses something, and does not pursue it.

Jason doesn't reply but springs onto the rock beside her and indicates for her to follow. The rocks are slippery because of the mat of seaweed that is still wet from the receding sea.

'Careful on this wet seaweed, it can be treacherous,' Jason warns her.

'These old tennis shoes have a really good grip, even in the wet!' she replies.

But she stumbles slightly and he takes her hand to help her across a narrow gully.

'Look at these incredible formations of the strata of the rocks. They were laid down millions of years ago!' he says with a sense of amazement.

'Well, I didn't think it was last week! We do have rocks in Australia, you know, probably older than here. Ayers Rock for example? Oh never mind!' She detects a blank look and follows him a few yards further.

Jason is not sure how he should take this confident girl who has suddenly appeared and ponders anxiously as he scrambles over to the next place he is hoping to find. But she is friendly, and one of the very few girls who has spoken to him since leaving his mixed junior school. He decides to see how she will enjoy her time on the rocks that he already likes so much.

'Three parallel gullies, well just fissures really, but we go here and look east, and under the weed should be a good hole,' he confides, and flicks back the dangling wrack.

There, in the scoop in the rock, is a fine crab, with its distinctive ochre brown shell and black-tipped claws. With an audience of Abby to perform to, he sneaks the tip of the hook over the shell and twists it slightly to grip a claw. With a firm steady pull, he lifts the crab from the hole and flicks it to his feet, where it grabs onto the thick weed.

At the same time, he dislodges a second crab underneath, and it tumbles into the shallow water swirling in the narrow cleft below. He jumps down sideways into the water and spots the creature scurrying away. With his right hand, he grabs deep into the water and manages to grip it firmly. He holds it aloft in triumph.

'Wow, you little whippersnapper! That was neat boy; two in one!' Abby cheers.

'And both a good size, hooray!' Jason almost shouts in return, as he tempts each with seaweed before snuggling them into his bag. 'My gosh, look how the tide's gone out; we can almost walk to the wreck.'

'Let's go there, it looks exciting,' Abby cries and they carefully navigate their way across the weedy rocks. The undulating area is punctuated with numerous potholes scoured by the relentless pounding of the sea. Each dark pool looks eerie, mysterious and threatening.

Jason leads, remembering every word from Joe. About fifty yards from the wreck, there is the parallel gully that runs the opposite way to the others. It is just too wide to jump across, even for the fittest person, and the deep smoky-green colour suggests it is very deep.

Jason makes his way across the rocks to the right, still remembering Joe's advice, and indeed finds the spot with a shelf in the rock on both sides, and he springs across the gap with ease. He detects a touch of hesitation from Abby and beckons with an outstretched arm. She reaches forward and clutches his hand firmly and in one leaps the gully, landing at Jason's feet. She grabs him around the waist, holding firmly.

'Thank you, a little scary that!'

He smiles back. 'You OK? Let's find another secret place.' He takes her hand and helps her onto a rounded rock where they sit for a few seconds. 'It's near here, I'm sure.'

He fumbles in the haversack for his compass to check his bearings. They cross to another rock that leads to a narrow string of humps and onto a rounded sea-battered rock stripped of its weed by the relentless waves.

He looks at the compass again. 'I'm sure that's it; this is really exciting! This is the most secret of all holes, and it's in the open sea, I'm sure it will be over there by those few clumps of horse-tail weed. I hope it's not too deep!'

The sky now has numerous high clouds moving quickly from the west and wavelets are forming, blowing straight at them and making vision into the water more difficult. Undeterred, Jason peers through the shallow water for the rocks that will take him to the most intriguing secret of all. Carefully prodding with the base of his hook and net, he moves slowly along the ridge until he can see the far side of the rounded rock. He now stands looking back to Abby, and just under the flecking wavelets, he can make out the dark entrance of a sort of tunnel in the rock.

'This must be it,' he whispers to Abby as though he might be overheard, and wades carefully through the deep water towards the foreboding darkness, leaving her safely on a rock. 'Now I see why Joe told me to have a long pole for the hook.' He nods to himself as he reaches forward and probes the tip of the hook into the recess. He reaches further and further until only a foot of the handle remains. He is now in front of the hole and almost waist deep in the cool water. 'There's a resident tapping the hook here!' he yells as he feels a gripping onto the metal and slowly, he withdraws the hook with something firmly attached. Through the murky, disturbed water, he spots a thick, dark-red antenna; then a second appears, waving as it senses the light.

'It's a lobster, a big lobster! Go away waves!' he cries as the ripples on the surface impair his vision. Then suddenly his hook twists violently in his hand and he loses his grip and frantically snatches to retrieve the pole. 'What the heck was that? The hook was pulled from me! Now the blinking lobster's gone, dash!' he shouts in frustration as he starts to feel the hook sliding back into the hole. The water is now cloudy, yet he continues with diligence to probe into the darkness for some movement. He reaches deeply then suddenly the hook twists sharply in his hand, but he holds on firmly.

'It's huge, whatever this is, it's *huge*!' he shouts at Abby, as he slowly withdraws the hook.

'Such excitement! How frightful!' She calls from her perch several yards away. 'What's happened to my quiet little boy! Thrill of the hunt eh?' she adds with a big grin.

He looks up and smiles then peers back into the now chafing water, but his concentration is immediately broken by the noise of a group of five scruffy young men making their way over the rocks towards them.

'Oh heck, I don't want them to see where I am; I'm sure they're the ones I saw in the village earlier taunting Joe, what a rough-looking lot,' he says to himself, hoping Abby will hear.

She does. 'Just stay there and pretend to be prodding with your net for prawns!' she suggests.

He nods. 'Maybe it will be better if I let the water clear for a minute. If only this wind would abate!'

He wades carefully back to Abby, pretending to fish for prawns with his net.

The five approaching males are in their late teens or early twenties, and are all thick set and dark-haired, except for the one with blonde hair who had kept away while the others taunted Joe. He wears a rugby shirt, shorts and boots. The others are in tattered ripped-off trousers rolled up above their knees. He knows they are the same gang for the blonde lad is distinctive. They stamp their way towards Jason and Abby, looking angry that someone is on their patch. They deliver a long, hard, unfriendly glare to the two of them. The five plunge into the deep parallel gully and out the other side without hesitation, marching aggressively towards the wreck, brandishing three long poles with great barbed hooks on the end.

'In ya go, Blondie, Kevin and Steve,' the boss of the group commands. His square angry face and unkempt long dark hair say not to mess or argue. Within seconds, there is much banging and muffled shouting with frequent sharp expletives. Then there's a muffled sort of bark as one boy's head appears from a gap in the side of the rounded stern of the rusting ship.

There are sharp exchanges then another boy's head sticks out from the hole with an excruciating expression of pain. He slowly pulls out a pole with much thrashing and swearing, and the head of a large conger eel emerges, impaled on the hook. The boss grabs the pole and yanks the writhing creature onto the rock, where his mate already has a large chunk of metal from near the wreck in his hand. They both bend down and the iron chunk crashes down on the eel's head, flattening it in one, spurting a shower of blood that splatters all over their clothes.

Within seconds, the blonde boy emerges and stands on the flat part of the metal and bends to receive another pole as it's heaved out.

'An even bigger eel!' reverberates from inside and the boy struggles to pull the huge slashing conger from the crack in the hull.

'Stone me, wot a mighty creature!' another shouts as the boss takes the pole and attempts to anchor the creature's powerful body to the rock with his hob-nailed boot. He stamps several times and slips backwards into the water. This sends him into a rage, and he shouts obscenities into the air.

'Hit the nasty thing hard!' he commands, and the lad crashes the metal towards the head of the conger, which writhes away at the last second. 'Hit it hard, I said!' he barks, and after much thrashing and banging, finally he gets a straight a blow to the head and follows it with another to the tail, close to the vent.

The eel still writhes defiantly. It is over six feet long and even thicker than the boss's stocky, muscular legs. It takes five further bashes to dispatch it. By this time, another pole has poked out and the blonde boy hands out a smaller conger that's about five feet, and this one is quickly dealt with.

The blonde boy clambers out with his clothes soaked and splashed with blood. Jason wonders why this boy, who didn't take part in taunting Joe, is part of this group of ruffians. The gang quickly string up the three eels, passing thick chord through the gills and mouth of each one to give a secure grip.

'What ya' catchin', boy?' one of them shouts to Jason.

'Prawns!' he replies, waving his net.

'Watch one of these doesn't get ya, have ya leg off in one,' he barks back, and they stamp back across the rocks and up a steep part of the cliff, dragging the three congers behind them.

'They do make me shudder with anger, those horrid people!' Jason says to Abby, remembering what they did to Joe that morning. 'Still I must try to catch this huge lobster before the tide comes in further!' He wades confidently back to his position in front of the rock, immediately plunging deeply with his hook.

'I can feel it, it's still here, but difficult to see. I think I've got it!' he says excitedly as he slowly begins to withdraw the hook from the depths, holding his net in his left hand ready to trap it. 'Yes, yes, yes, it's coming, it's coming. Nearly there!' With great care, he pulls his hook clear of the hole in the very murky water. He brings it towards his net, his face transfixed in expectation.

'Dash, dash, it got off, bother it!' he yells, and he plunges the net deep with vain hope. This clouds the water further and several larger wavelets surge around him. He plunges his hook back into the hole, and feels a solid twist. 'Got it again!' But the pole slips from his grasp. He lunges to retrieve it and slips sideways, then disappears totally under the water. Abby gasps. But in a moment, Jason surfaces, firmly on his feet. He gasps and shakes his head, then clasps his hook and somewhat unsteadily gets back in front of the hole to try again. Frantically, he tries to hook the creature, but the surging waves make it even more difficult.

'Blinking sea, get back, bother the sea!' he bellows in frustration, and Abby cannot help but laugh. 'Don't you laugh!' he shouts at her as he tries to regain composure, but the water is now above his waist and he is struggling to keep a foothold.

'Jason, please accept that whatever that is, it's in its true element, and you will be too, if you don't give up! Sorry, but it's true! Old King Canute couldn't do it!' she says with a pleading expression.

Dejected and wet, Jason now faces the wade back to Abby, who is looking quite concerned. Step by step, he shuffles through the deep water using his crab hook as a wading staff. Relieved, he pulls himself from the depths onto the rock alongside her.

'Never mind!' she comforts, 'you've got some super crabs, I'm proud of you!' She hugs his shivering body. 'Heck mate, we must get back and quick, look at the tide; it's covering the rocks. Quick, quick!'

He nods, gasping for breath, and they plunge through the oncoming sea and scramble to the relative safety of the slippery rocks, not stopping until they feel safe on higher rocks. They continue to the base of the cliff where Jason left his dry clothes.

'Well, that was an adventure!' he says.

'Certainly was, but sorry, must be off—friends will wonder where the heck I am. You OK? I'll see you again!' she smiles.

'Oh I do hope so!' he smiles too and laughs. 'I'll be somewhere around here the next three days while the tides last. Come again, and thank you for your company!' He proffers his hand which she shakes with a laugh, and then she climbs the track up towards the cliff path.

As he watches her climb, he considers how lucky he was to meet her. She seems friendly and open, and he thinks how much nicer she is compared to others of his age at home. It has been a fun hour with her. *If only I had the same kind of chums at home!* He is thinking of all the questions he is subjected to: why doesn't he do this, play that game, mix as all others do…his mind drifts away.

Jason takes a swig of squash from his lunch pack, ponders a while, then walks around a corner to look back towards the far point to see it from a different perspective. Perhaps this is what he should do with his own life. Then he spots a shallow pool and he slowly wades around it.

In the distance on the shingle in the inlet, two younger boys appear to be searching amongst the stones.

Are they a threat, he wonders, but decides to carry on anyway. He looks back at a muddy corner of the pool and paddles over towards it. From a small hole just above the water line, he can see the head of an eel sticking out, its mouth gaping wide. It appears stranded out of the pool. He splashes water at it and the creature jerks upwards for a second. It is obviously alive and he gets his hook and positions himself carefully, standing on two boulders. Now he can reach the hole while keeping his feet out of the water.

He puts the hook inside the mouth of the eel that appears to be moribund, and jerks it downwards. The eel springs to life and tenses its body, raising its fins in aggression. Steadily, Jason drags, inch by inch, the awakened slimy body from the hole. It lashes around as it touches the surface of the pool, then with a final heave, Jason pulls it totally from its refuge. It's nearly four feet long, the slender canine head belying the girth of its body. Thrashing its head it wriggles free from the hook and swims around in the shallow water.

He stands and watches the elegant swimming of the eel, as though oblivious to the injury Jason has inflicted on it, flicking its tail in rhythm either side and propelling the alert raised head forward. It blunders into the shallow water and begins thrashing as though confused. Jason leaps over towards it and slides the tip of the hook underneath its belly and yanks it towards the dry rocks. The metal bends and the eel slips off and squirms and slithers back to the water, then swims into a deeper part of the pool. Seconds later, it re-emerges from under some hanging weed as Jason positions himself with a large chunk of rock to bombard the creature.

Seeing activity the two boys, who are much the same age as Jason, make their way over just as Jason drops the stone on the eel swimming underneath him. The blow is cushioned by the water, but it is partially stunned. Jason seizes another stone, his enthusiasm fired by the new challenge, and he hurls it into the water towards the eel. His endeavours before the watching lads make them laugh, as he pretends to be an experienced fisher of the rocks. He yells in excitement as he successfully manages to stun the eel with the second stone, and then he is able to lodge the hook into its gills and pull the tiring creature fully from the water onto a patch of shingle. He crashes another large stone onto its head and at last the battle has been won. The boys cheer and examine the eel with Jason.

'It's huge. I've never seen an eel like that!' says the younger lad, as the other nods in agreement.

'Well, you should have seen the enormous ones some men caught in the wreck, out there,' Jason points. 'They had huge gaffs to pull them out. One eel was longer than you!' he says to the older lad, 'and it was *this* thick!' he indicates with both hands.

Both lads are taken aback by Jason's vivid description. The elder looks at Jason quizzically. 'Do you live here? We are from Manchester, but are here staying with our cousin for Easter. He has a cold so can't come out. My name's Nicholas and this is my brother Roger. And yours?'

Jason looks at them both, thinking they have a sort of admiration for his agility and skill, and for the fine catch he has landed. He feels proud.

'It's Jason, but I don't live here either,' he smiles. 'I am staying with Uncle and Aunt for the holiday. I have caught four crabs as well,' he boasts, then thinks he is giving away his secrets too readily. 'But please keep that a secret. I don't want everyone to know what I have caught. So shush!' he says putting his index finger to his lips.

'We were told to come here to look for shells, just look,' says Roger, wriggling his hand from a trouser pocket. He splays his palm to show several elegant cowrie shells, and his brother does the same.

Not quite the same as my catch, Jason thinks proudly to himself, but smiles at them, admiring the beautiful symmetrical pink shells.

'Come on, Rog, we must go. We've been nearly two hours and we've been warned about the dangerous tides here, so don't want Aunty to be worried. Nice to meet you, Jason, maybe see you around in the next week?' says Nicholas. They scramble over the rocks and up the cliff, turning to wave several times, to which Jason responds enthusiastically.

He picks up the conger to assess its weight. It must be six to eight pounds, he decides. 'Four crabs and a conger!' he shouts to the sky once they are out of earshot, then washes himself in a pool and stands on a rock to dry in the light breeze, glad of the sun's gentle heat. He gazes out to sea then at his bulging haversack, enjoying every second of freedom and success. Soon, he is totally dry and he pulls on his lovely dry shorts and pullover, gathers his tackle and catch and makes his way up the cliff, dragging the conger on his hook behind him, following the earlier example of the rough men pulling their three congers across the rocks. He feels proud of his catch, even though he knows that it was a very brutal way to achieve it; it certainly was a very exciting few minutes, and he has triumphed.

On the cliff path, he passes several people taking a walk, all of whom comment favourably on his catch. He likes the admiration and continues to feel elated. Two men, laden with fishing rods and tackle, are observing the flooding tide, planning their evening of fishing. One of them takes some strong string from his bag and ties the conger securely in a ring so it is easy for Jason to carry. They see his excitement and congratulate him and he thanks them profusely. He springs confidently around the path back to Longbeach and continues up through the woodland steps. He swaps hands carrying the conger every five minutes to relieve his muscles of the tiring weight. In little over thirty minutes, he is back at his uncle's house, and though exhausted, he has a most satisfied beam on his face.

There is great excitement at the catch and Uncle calls in his friendly neighbours the Joneses to admire it. Wiry, bespectacled and bald, Mr Jones has a warm aura and beaming face. He pats Jason several times on the back as Jason relates how he caught the eel. Mrs Jones, a prim lady with wavy grey hair, advises Jason to take the conger to Mrs Betty, an eccentric who lives in the end house in Milk Lane on the edge of Crescent Woods, not too far away.

'For your first-time out fishing, you seem to be an expert already!' remarks Mr Jones, as Jason blushes.

'Mrs Betty will be pleased, for she has a special recipe for baked eel, and she will look after you!' Mrs Jones assures him.

Enthused by their admiration, Jason then tells of another experience. 'I was prawning out towards the wreck, and five big men, armed with huge gaffs, hooked out three huge congers, far, far bigger than this one.'

'Sounds like the lot from East End Farm,' Mr Jones says. 'Certainly, they're a rough lot. Most probably those eels will end up as food for their pigs.'

After the Joneses depart, Uncle Charles looks at Jason seriously. 'Hear this, Gert!' he calls to his wife. 'We thought you were only to be on the rocks in the middle of Longbeach, not around at Blackledge?' he says to Jason, who realises his enthusiasm had caused him to let out where exactly he had been on the rocks. He looks ashamed.

Then hesitantly he says, 'It was Mr Joe who told me Blackledge was the best place for crabs, and exactly how to get there. He even described the rocks, the gullies, pools and many of the holes. That's how I managed to catch these four crabs, in his holes.'

'Well, he knows the place better than anyone. It's unusual for him to share his knowledge so willingly. He must have taken a shine to you. In his younger days, he was very abrupt, even rude, to many people. Some of those who remember that side of him now might tease the old boy since he's too frail to defend himself.'

'But Jason, the cliffs are dangerous in places!' Aunty cuts in. 'You were not supposed to go there!'

'I know, Aunty, but I do know all the key rules of rock climbing— Dad showed me when we were walking and climbing the hills. I know not ever to climb above your own height without a rope! The path down to Blackledge is easy, not dangerous like other places. I assure you I am very careful. And I am a very good swimmer as I know my parents have assured you.'

'All right, we'll leave it there,' says Uncle. 'I can see that already you are fuelled by the challenges here.'

'Yes, indeed,' says Jason, relieved. Then he has a concerned expression. 'But Uncle, I saw some men teasing Joe this morning. They were really horrid to him!'

'Ah, that'll most likely be the lot from East End Farm. There has been a family feud running for years, indeed generations. It'll continue till they see him in his grave, and beyond. Just don't get involved in it. That's my advice.'

'It was the same people who caught the congers at Blackledge,' Jason shakes his head, thinking to himself how he has already become involved in the feud, and has the bruise to show for it, which he aims to keep covered and out of sight.

The early evening is spent cooking the crabs, then Aunty prepares supper. At the table, Uncle Charles carves a piece of ham. Jason comes in having taken a quick bath and now feels refreshed.

'What a lovely smell!' he enthuses. 'A favourite of mine!'

'It seems all food is your favourite!' Charles laughs. 'You have a good appetite, so I don't know why you are so thin; nowt wrong with you though!' He laughs. 'How was the rest of your day, Jason?'

'I couldn't believe it. So many places Joe described were all there. He was amazingly accurate! The biggest crab was in a hole exactly as he said. I even found what he calls the secret hole, but the sea was too deep to catch the big lobster that was there. Still, it's a nice catch of crabs for us to enjoy,' he says, feeling quite pleased with himself.

At that moment, Aunty comes in with a bowl of mashed potatoes, another of bright green cabbage, and a third brimming with dappled-green parsley sauce. 'Here, we have ham from Rees the butcher, and Savoy cabbage from the garden,' she announces.

'Gosh! The sauce tastes so fresh,' Jason says, licking his lips.

'Uncle always keeps parsley for the winter in the greenhouse, so in the spring it grows quickly and tastes exquisite, perfect for a parsley sauce!' Gertie says, pouring a pool of it onto the side of her plate.

While they eat, Jason continues to tell them both of his exciting day, the disappointment of not catching the big lobster and then the drama of landing the conger, but he decides not to mention Abby just yet. He does confirm he will take the conger to Mrs Betty early in the morning.

After supper, Jason begins to fall asleep from the excitement and exhaustion of his day. In his room, he kneels to say his prayers as he does every night. After his routine that ends with The Lord's Prayer, he looks at the bruise on his arm that Uncle and Aunt have not seen, kneels again and slowly says:

'Please Lord, forgive my bad language today as I did get over-excited. Also, I forgive Mr Joe for hitting me on the arm, for as Jesus said on the Cross, he didn't know what he was doing. So please forgive him as I do. It was the sad rage of a bullied and tormented old man. Poor Old Joe.'

He climbs into bed and immediately falls into a deep dream-filled sleep.

Sea Belt

Chapter Four

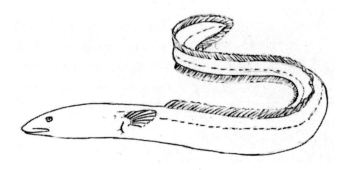

Conger Eel

A Big Pool

At six in the morning, the sun is beaming and the bay shimmers with golden light. When Jason awakes from his sound sleep, he looks at the bright view from his window and immediately begins to plan his day. He has to get to see Mrs Betty before she goes to work at eight, and he wants to take a dressed crab to Joe, as he is sure it will make him happy. He must do this before setting off for the rocks and, as low tide is quarter past two, he aims to be there two hours before, so the morning will go quickly.

He takes the largest of the cow crabs from the fridge and thinks how very different it is from the crab he has had at home. He has only seen it in tins and tasted it from small pots, spread on bread and butter, or in a sandwich.

He sets a double piece of newspaper on the kitchen table.

Aunty Gertie has shown him exactly how to dress a crab and because of his almost photographic memory knows every step of the procedure. He tugs at the carapace to separate it from the body and legs. It parts easily as the shoulders are almost splitting naturally in preparation for ecdysis, when the crab casts the old shell and emerges larger with a soft shell. He knows this from reading his *Pocket Guide to the Seashore.* His face lights up as he admires the shell bulging with firm pale yellow to pink meat.

He pulls out the dead men's fingers, or gills, some of which are attached to the centre inner shell, or honeycomb, together with some fine cellular membranes. He presses the jaw that is linked to the back shell, or carapace, below the eyes. It breaks with a sharp click then he eases out the stomach, often called the purse, which contains the remnants of the crab's last meal. With a round-tipped table knife, he eases the dark meat from the carapace and it reveals a complete impression of the new shell that is fully developed within the existing one.

Carefully, he takes the centre body and bends the claws backwards to remove them together with the bottom knuckle, revealing the succulent white meat of the body. He repeats with all the legs, putting them in a neat mound. Using a part-opened hair grip, he eases out the white meat from each part of the honeycomb, and separates the claws and legs into individual joints. Precisely, he cracks each base leg joint with the nut cracker and eases each long tender muscle in one with the hair clip. He bangs the end claw joint with the folded nut cracker to just break the shell so he can take out the meat in its impressive bulbous shape. It has the ochre hue of the shell and beneath is the finest white meat.

He arranges all the pickings artistically back into the shell, topping it with the two fat claws. Meticulously, he wraps the shell in a piece of greased bread paper, securing it with a binding of raffia tied in a bow. He slips it into a brown paper bag and puts it in the Kelvinator fridge.

He creeps into the back yard and opens the coal-house door to see the conger eel hanging head to tail in a ring and shudders as he sees a small pool of blood below. The large yellow eyes, dark slate-brown body and silver belly still look somewhat menacing in the dark of the shed, and he closes the door. He looks down at the garden at all the fresh vegetables and muses that he has rarely seen these growing. At home, they usually have these from a tin.

Quietly, he goes back upstairs to wash and dress, not wishing to disturb Aunty and Uncle early on a Saturday morning, and by seven-thirty he is well on his way. He feels proud carrying the conger as he strides up the road to visit the mysterious Mrs Betty in her house on the edge of the village by Crescent Woods.

Mrs Jones described the route through the village, in the opposite direction from the beach, and up a gentle hill called Milk Lane. From the brow of the hill, the lane descends a short while to the small woods, and the row of cottages on the right is where Mrs Betty lives. The trees are just coming into leaf and their fresh lime-green foliage casts eerie shadows over the interior of the woods, where swathes of the first bluebells of the spring shimmer in the gentle breeze.

Jason puts any alarmist thoughts away and marches briskly on. The sharp yap of a terrier echoes through the woods, punctuated by the occasional deep guttural growl from something much larger. It gets louder as he approaches the cottages and rather nervously, he walks quickly to the gate of the end garden. It is about ten yards to the front door and either side of the path is planted with rows of vegetables, similar to Uncle Charles's garden. A small wisteria over the front porch is just about to burst into festoons of mauve flowers. He marvels at how advanced all plants here seem to be compared with those in his home area.

He knocks just once and it is answered by a lady of medium height with mid-brown wavy hair, a plump frame, and florid face that smiles in a friendly way.

'Mrs Betty?' he enquiries politely.

She can see what he is holding half behind him. 'Did you catch that? It's a beauty, a very nice size,' she replies in a soft ringing voice with quite a cultured accent.

'Yes I did, yesterday afternoon. It's been kept cool all night. Mrs Jones, our neighbour, said you might like it.'

'Oh, yes, indeed! Give it here and I'll put it in the kitchen. How much do you want for it?' she says, holding it up high as she waddles back into the house.

He thinks to himself, should I say sixpence, a shilling, or what? 'Oh really, it's up to you. I've no idea of the price. I'm pleased for you to have it,' he says hesitantly, as she returns holding a red Welsh wool tapestry purse.

'Here, I hope this is enough!' She proffers a half crown and she can see he is happy as his face lights up. 'I'd ask you in for a cup of tea, but I'm off to work at the hotel in the East Bay. Been there for years. They say I'm part of the family. But I'm the only one who likes eel; all types of eels. It's because eels grow very slowly and build up lots of fat and reserves in their body, so the meat, which is pure white, is absolutely delicious.'

She pauses a moment as she contemplates the pleasure of eating it.

'If you ever get river eels, let me know, but there are no streams here. Because the area is limestone rock, the water goes underground and then makes the wet patches on beaches where it emerges. The only place to catch them is the little brook where the stream emerges in the dry valley, where it runs for about half a mile before it enters the sea, but it's a very long walk as no roads go there. Beautiful place though. It's my favourite. You also have very good crabbing on the rocks as no one goes there either; then trout and eels in the stream, as many as you want.'

She laughs. 'I'm sorry I'm talking too much, I must go as I'm never late for work. Thank you very much. And if you catch some big crabs, the hotel will buy them. I'll speak to the chef. And watch that dog two doors down. He's a real bully, argues and fights with any other dog. If a walker passes by, look out.'

She bustles away cheerily, as Jason walks slowly and pensively up the garden path to the gate hoping he will not encounter the dog. Suddenly, from behind, he hears a "Psss" and turns to see Mrs Betty beckoning to him.

'Listen, never be worried by bullies, whether dogs or people. I sorted that bully dog out, and many others. I always carry this!' She pulls a small yellow cylindrical tub from her bag. 'Lion white pepper, but any pepper will do. Give it a blooming good shake over them. Ha, ha! You'll get them sneezing and then the pepper sticks in their hair and infuriates them. When they scratch, it gets them sneezing again. They'll not bother you after that.'

She giggles again. 'Same with bully boys. One night, three followed me. Don't know what they wanted but I didn't trust them. I'd been paid that night, so with the three around me I gave them a good dousing of pepper. You should have seen them! Sneezing and wiping their eyes. They never bother me now. Thought I'd tell you. Bye now. And she returns to her house, having sensed that Jason is nervous of other people.

He walks briskly up the rough road to the brow, taking care not to attract the bully dog as it yelps and growls from inside the end house.

He walks back quickly, hoping Joe will be in his usual spot so he can present him with the dressed cow crab. Slightly out of breath, he turns a corner to see Joe with two walking sticks shuffling down the pavement. He sits and gazes, sniffing the morning air. As it is Saturday, already many people are walking down the gentle hill to the shops. Several stop to acknowledge Joe and he raises his arm waving in a friendly gesture. He recognises many of the voices but his feeble sight means he cannot focus clearly on their faces.

'Good Morning, Mr Joe!' Jason calls in a cheery voice, 'it's Jason, and my hook works really well, thank you. Yesterday, I caught four crabs and a small conger, so here is the dressed cow crab I promised you!' And he stretches out his arms, almost touching Joe, who clasps his thin wrist with his weather-beaten right hand.

'Ya mean tis for me, a cow crab?' he says, feeling the grease-proof paper package. 'Nice size too, ya's a nice lad, most boys is 'orrid, 'orrid, all! Please take it to Mr David inside, man with beard.'

'Yes, Mr Joe, I've already met him.'

'Oh good, ask him to put in fridge for Joe. Say it's for my tea. Thank ye, lad.'

Once he has done this, Jason comes back to the old man's side and says, enunciating clearly, 'Also I found the secret hole near the wreck; nobody else went near it, but I found it. And there was a huge lobster...'

Joe suddenly perks up and almost looks alert. 'Ya really did catch it?'

'Hmmm, not quite, I'm afraid—there was a choppy sea. I could feel it and nearly had it to the net. Saw its two long red feelers through the murk. It was so strong it almost pulled me in!'

'Sure wasn't a big old conger? Often share a hole ya know. Like a powerful rubbery twist, strong and firm...'

Jason frowns in concentration. 'Well, yes, I guess it might have been, but today, it's calm and the tide is lower so I'll look again at slack tide. Something else happened, Joe. Five rough boys pulled three huge congers from the wreck...'

'They'll be from East End Farm, a rough lot indeed. Load of bullies. Watch them; nick ya catch given a chance. Pick a fight then nick it, devils. End up with no catch and a black eye, careful. Boys is 'orrid!' Joe growls from the back of his croaky throat. 'Go now so ya early for tide. Oh! Ta so much for crab, ta, lad. And watch for conger, bullies of the undersea world, bullies to all, hunt anything on the sea bed.'

Jason trots the short way home in a happy yet pensive mood. It seems the place is full of bullies. Horrid boys, dogs, congers; what else? Deep inside, he hopes he will not see a bully again, ever.

As he arrives home just after nine, he can detect the aroma of sizzling bacon. Aunty has laid the breakfast, and the same smell induces Uncle to come in from the garden.

'Did you meet Mrs Betty?' she asks Jason as she pours the tea.

'Yes, she's very nice,' he replies. 'She seemed very pleased with the eel. She's a fascinating lady!'

Aunty presents the plates, each with three rashers of bacon and two pieces of grilled tomato, and puts a basket of brown toast and a bowl of butter in the middle of the table. They eat heartily with many nods of approval.

'Come on,' Uncle jests, 'how much did she give you for it? They say she's a mean old dear!'

'Gosh, no! Far from it. She gave me half a crown! And some advice,' Jason picks up the yellow tub of pepper, pauses a second, then says, 'Now, I can repay you for the hook, Aunty.'

'No, indeed, Jason, that was a present from us to you. Put the money in your savings.'

'What advice did she give you?' Uncle enquires.

'Oh, yes, she said to use pepper to deter bullies, dogs and people. A good shake of pepper gets them all sneezing!' he laughs.

'Nay, Jason!' Charles says firmly, 'I don't suggest that at all. It's hardly a pleasant thing to do to a dog, and I saw an owner get very cross and aggressive when a teenager did it to his Jack Russell. The boy thought he was in for it. And do it to ruffians and they might turn on you. So be warned. I'd forget this *advice*, now!'

'Now, what time are you leaving, as we take it you are going to the rocks again? I have to pack your food,' Aunty cuts in to change the subject, seeing Jason's reaction to Charles's words.

'Yes, of course! I'd like to leave around ten thirty, so I'm in plenty of time. Is that convenient for you both?' Jason replies.

'That's fine. Now you can finish writing that letter home and be off in good time,' she says, pointing with a smile to the stairs, and Jason goes to his room.

When the letter is written, he gets ready for the exciting day ahead. As he pulls on his swimming trunks, he feels that his leg muscles are already becoming slightly firmer from the exercise on the rocks and stands flexing his small muscles in front of the mirror for several minutes. He clenches his fists and tightens his thin biceps. He stretches his body to full height. *This is the life I want,* he thinks. *The natural exercise on the rocks will tone up my body.* He feels that perhaps even the puny Jason is growing up.

His thoughts flash back to the mean names he has been called in school. But then he tries hard to banish those memories and concentrates on the achievements of the last few days and the open-air life he now knows he loves. He hopes he can soon shake off and forget the spiteful treatment of the past, hard though he knows that will be.

Soon, walking briskly, having followed the bus route again, he is making his way down the steps of Parson's Wood with new-found confidence. He arrives on Longbeach to find that already groups of people are gathering, arranging deck chairs in clusters, rows and circles. He senses they are looking at him. Although he is early for the tide, his unease returns and he runs all the way across the beach, determined to avoid them, then on to the coastal path from Traxi Point to Blackledge.

He now slows down to a brisk walk and soon arrives at the iron pillars, then carefully descends the path down to the rocks. There is one person already on there who seems to be searching for something in the large pools. I thought I would be first today. Well, that can't be helped, he thinks, summoning up a new-found bravery. I won't be deterred.

Jason strips to his trunks and as usual, hides his clothes and lunch pack. The sun is remarkably warm on his body. Suddenly, as he idles across to a large pool, he spots two more people with hooks appearing from the further side where the strata shelve to a large sandy beach. He slings his haversack over a shoulder and slowly makes his way to the tide line, brandishing his hook and net in anticipation, yet he is a touch wary of the deeper-looking pools.

He gazes into each that he passes. He observes many of the shallow pools have lots of different shells of various shapes and sizes strewn amongst the stones and shingle. His eye soon sets on many old oyster shells, whelks, mussels, top shells, cockles and other clams, as well as the remains of crab carapaces. One oyster shell has a brighter, more vivid colour than others and he plunges in to retrieve it. As soon as he clasps the round flat shell, he realises from its weight that it is full, the only live one amongst all the debris. He holds it to the sky, then wraps it in some oar weed and slips it into his bag.

His keen eyes fix on the gentle waves, watching for the first signs of the parallel gully. He wonders if the people he saw in the distance to the west will come to this area, but is pleased to see the other person he saw has gone towards the west; he looks over, shrugs, and decides to carry on anyway.

He works along a fissure that has many nooks where smaller crabs can hide. In one large recess in an awkward corner, he feels a decent-sized crab and flexes his body into a contortion that enables him to reach the carapace. After a few minutes of tugging and wrestling, the creature comes free; it is a nice bull crab. Behind is a smaller yet still sizeable cow which he pulls out easily. Its legs are neatly folded—a sign that it is about to cast its shell. He wraps both of them in seaweed and puts them with the oyster in the haversack.

The wreck is now well proud of the water and the gully distinctive, yet perhaps too deep to cross safely. The other two crabbers have now moved closer but are engrossed in trying to trap something in a deep pool. He ignores them and makes his way cautiously to where he can cross, hoping that he can get to his secret hole before anyone else.

As he day-dreams whether the inhabitants will still be there, he wonders how an elegant eel could be a bully. Indeed, *he* felt the bully when the rock crashed onto the head of the eel the day before. However, it was all over very quickly, it was for food after all, and he earned a half-crown from it. He gazes up at the sky then down to the water lapping the seaweed-strewn rocks; the water is draining away rapidly.

Already, he can leap across the gully and head towards the hole. He wades very carefully and fortunately, the clear water makes it far simpler than on the previous day, and quickly, he reaches the small outcrop that marks his secret hole.

He perches on top of the rock right next to the hole and, holding firmly to the roots of a clump of oar weed, he eases forward, with arched back, to peer through the water directly into the entrance. Here, the water is slightly discoloured, and his nose is almost touching its surface by the time he is able to look into the tunnel. Then a surge of water drops away and just a few inches from him is the nose of a huge black eel, far bigger than the one he caught, with two enormous yellow eyes with pitch- black round pupils. It is motionless but Jason rears back, almost losing his grip, fearing it could attack at any second.

His heart is beating fast and, keeping more of a distance, he again stares directly at the great quivering jaws. Gradually, he can appreciate the huge size of the eel as the particles in the water settle. It has a vast head—to him is the size of a black Labrador. Heaven knows how long the body is, he shudders to himself.

'I name him Jack, after the famous beach dog who rescued many swimmers from drowning,' he shouts into the air. Then, with the base of the hook, he knocks several large cone-shaped limpets from the rocks. Underneath each is the grey-green sucker that holds it to the rocks, with strange stumpy antennae either side of an oval mouth. Using his thumb nail, he quickly loosens one from its shell revealing its bulbous black liver and guts. He stretches over the water and drops it into the entrance of the hole. It sinks rapidly then the dark shape of the conger surges forward and back again.

A second limpet, he dangles on the surface, holding it with trepidation. The great head inches forward as Jason drops it nervously.

He sees the conger suck it into its opened mouth then settle down again. Jason drops a further limpet, and again, the conger eases forward and takes it gently. *He likes to be fed,* Jason thinks. *Treat him nicely and he is not a bully at all.*

His concentration is disturbed when he hears a girl's voice calling him, and looking up he sees Abby heading his way. As she approaches, he calls in a low voice, 'Come and see Jack, the enormous conger, it's huge, really huge, I'm not kidding!'

'Gee, I was very stiff after crossing the rocks yesterday, particularly this morning.' She mimes an old-person's stretch. 'How were you this morning?'

'I was up early. I caught a conger after you went and a lady called Mrs Betty gave me two and six for it. What about that? There's a huge one here, I'll show you. As I said, he's called Jack, and we aren't catching him. I've been feeding him limpets. He likes them. He must be very old, he's enormous!'

Jason loosens another limpet and drops it into the water as they both squat to see if the conger will take it. Again, it creeps forward and grabs the mollusc in one moment.

'Wow, that's big, see what you mean!' She watches, fascinated. 'But look, something else is there.' She peers into the water in set concentration. 'My gad!' suddenly she calls, not moving an inch. 'Those red antennae and big blue body, so blue you've never seen such blue! Look, look!'

Jason crouches alongside her; both are mesmerised by the crustacean as a shard of sunlight catches the entrance of the hole, igniting the true blue of its wondrous exoskeleton. 'It's a lobster, and a jolly big one too,' Jason whispers.

'I name her Matilda!' Abby says proudly. 'She's is too beautiful to catch as well. Her shell is the colour of the night sky, in Oz that is, where the Southern Cross shines brightly. Here, no colour matches that, only her. We'll guard them both. They're our chums.'

Jason nods, and looks up. 'Oh heavens, look who's coming with those big barbed hooks. It's the lot who were here yesterday. We must pretend to be prawning. If they see Jack, he'll be yanked out ruthlessly like the others. They are the real bullies round here. Quick, let's go over there,' he says, grabbing her hand.

They move several yards inshore and Jason runs his net underneath over-hanging clumps of weed. He sees something dart away and lifts the net to see several large prawns jumping amongst the weed. Abby, without flinching, grabs them firmly, holding each by the proboscis as the tail flaps furiously. She drops them into his haversack and he plunges the net in again.

A quick glance confirms what Jason had feared—they are indeed the ones he saw catching eels on the wreck yesterday, the same ones who were taunting Joe. They trudge to the wreck once more and one slides his body through the gap in the side. After much shouting and banging, he passes the butt of the gaff through the slit and the other one heaves a conger out onto the slippery rocks, where it is quickly dispatched. However, it's not much larger than the one Jason caught.

'Nothing else but prawns! Boy, plenty of tiddlers in 'ere, prawns for ya, 'ere!' The younger blonde one hollers at Jason, who looks up and waves cautiously in acknowledgement. Then they move further away and prod under some chunks of metal piping, and other parts that have broken off the main body of the wreck.

There is a loud cheer and a scream as one of them pulls another conger from a pipe and they gather around to admire it. Their second catch is also summarily battered to death and Jason shivers as he imagines the same fate might ensue for the mighty Jack. He is so pleased when they move away, stamping through the pools and dragging the two corpses behind them.

It is a relief to see them climbing the cliff, and when the they are out of sight, Jason and Abby return to the hole with more limpets they've prised off the rocks. It is approaching low tide and the water is now only a foot deep, and the slithery back of the great conger can be seen disappearing into its tunnel. As before, it takes the limpets as gently as a soft-mouthed retriever, crunching them in a gulp. Then a whispery red feeler appears and a dark-blue shape emerges. It gets brighter as it creeps from the shadow of the hole.

'Isn't she beautiful, such a vibrant dazzle, wow!' Abby enthuses as they peer down, shoulder to shoulder. 'Why *she*?' Jason replies a tad indignantly.

'Look, her tail is wide, but the claws are quite small compared to those of a cock! We call them cock and hen, not bull and cow. Bet she has eggs under the tail, thousands of them festooned like myriads of tiny black pearls. She's waiting patiently for them to hatch. Hope nobody catches her. They are the future lobsters of these rocks. It's important to protect their safety.'

Abby confidently knocks several more limpets from the rocks and scoops them from their conical shells with her thumb. The conger gulps most but the lobster does take one, clutching it with its front legs that have small pincers for feeding. Then it slowly sinks back into the darkness.

'So why are you sure the conger is a he? You call him Jack!' Abby says confidently. Jason goes a little quiet, then suddenly Abby cocks her head in concentration. 'Well, it certainly looks masculine,' she concedes. 'But can you hear the tide turning? Listen to the water gurgling through the wreck. Let's zip there quickly to catch some prawns. That thug said there were *loads* there. Come on!' she stares directly at Jason, detecting his hesitation.

'I'm not sure if I like that place, it's eerie, particularly with that noise of water gurgling through the pipework.'

'Come on, little boy. It's quite safe!' she says, pulling his hand, and he regrets his moment of nervousness.

'Yes,' he says. 'Let's try it!'

The wreck towers over them; the iron, blackened from years under the sea, is gnarled and rough with encrustations—large barnacles, tube worms, mussels and all—that are covered with many different varieties of colourful seaweed. They perch on a rock at the side of the wreck and Jason wriggles his net under a corner of iron. It comes up jumping with many lively prawns and Abby manages to grab nearly all of them with her splayed fingers, dumping them into the haversack, but a few flick themselves free back into the sea. Jason dives the net down again and another good catch comes up. His enthusiasm now takes over and he contorts to get the net as deep as possible, scraping the corners under the water. The first wavelet of the flooding tide soaks him over the waist but he continues without any fear.

After twenty minutes, the bag is almost half full. It's a magnificent catch, but the sea has quietly flooded around them. They look at one another with a slight anxiety but step by step, they wade through the water the deepest of which is almost up to their bellies. Treading carefully they get back to the deep gully, turn and look towards the hole where Jack and Matilda are now safe below the waves and smile at one another. Jason slips as he jumps across, plunging armpit deep, but in seconds he is on the other side and without hesitation he helps Abby leap the gap and they carry on towards the higher rocks.

They walk up a cleft that leads them to a shallow pool and he realises it's where he caught the large crab the day before. In his excitement, he forgot to look there earlier. He crouches down and pulls back the wrack that covers the hole. When he peers inside, no crab is evident, but something dark is buried deeply in the black mud inside the tunnel. With a wiggle and twist of his hook, he lifts the dark object from the silt and it begins to move. Another twist and two large claws come flailing angrily forwards.

'Heavens, it's a lobster, look!' he cries.

They both stare as he manoeuvres the hook to drag the crustacean from the muddy hole. Out of water, it has far less agility, yet Jason has to be quick as soon the sea will flood the pool. The lobster flaps its tail repeatedly and it quickly slides into the water where immediately its agility is restored.

'Hurry, the tide's comin' in!' Abby says, looking at the water in the pool which is beginning to cloud as the tide surges in.

Jason's full of concentration, and is set on getting the lobster into his net. *Remember what Joe told me,* he thinks to himself. *Put the net behind the lobster, not in front, then the hook a foot ahead of it.* He does this and immediately it flaps its tail, sending it backwards into the trap.

Quickly, Jason raises the net from the water and the mud-splattered creature is safely in the depths of the mesh. Carefully, he dunks it in the water and as the lobster flexes its tail again, washing the mud from its dirty shell, it reverts to a deep blue.

71

'What a cock, look at those claws! Altogether a fine creature!' Abby enthuses.

Jason stands and holds the net up, his broad smile saying everything. 'A lobster! Not putting *this* one back! What you reckon? It's a beauty!'

'Clever little devil!' Abby laughs, as she holds the haversack open and Jason carefully puts a handful of weed on top of the prawns.

Tentatively, he picks up the lobster, clutching the carapace firmly behind the claws. The creature snaps angrily as carefully he guides it into the haversack tail first and settles it onto the rest of his catch. He places a further handful of weed on top to keep it moist.

'See, nobody knows my secret holes, and they must remain a secret. Quick, let's look at the one over here!' He leaps across several yards and flicks the weed back. His face lights up again. A magnificent crab. 'Now, that's why we call it a bull. Look, it's like the great flat head of a charging bull and those black claw tips are just like the horns. See what I mean?' With the confidence of an expert, he flicks the crustacean from the hole, and grabs it with his left hand. 'This is what Joe calls a dull old bull. It doesn't have a mate, so spends time just feeding, lucky thing.' Jason just manages to fit the crab into the haversack which is now full. He stretches the straps to the buckles to close it securely, and slings it on his shoulder.

Triumphantly, yet still wet, they return to the base of the cliff face where Jason hid his clothes.

'I packed an extra piece of chocolate and sandwich; I was hoping you might come!' he says happily. He offers Abby a sandwich which she eagerly accepts, and they sit and munch away. After a short while, she notices the mark on his arm, glances at his face with a quizzical gaze, but he shrugs his shoulders.

'Come on, another of those secrets?' she asks.

He looks down and shakes his head. 'I was just in the wrong place. I was whacked by mistake; it should have been that ruffian who was taunting...' And his voice trails off. 'But I just want to forget it. Thanks for asking though.'

'Open up with all secrets, it always feels better, really!' she concludes, smiling encouragingly at him.

He smiles in return, but doesn't say anything for a moment.

'Take some prawns and the crab home?' he offers.

'If I was in Oz, definitely, but these relations would think I'm trying to poison them; they've no idea at all, really. And saying that, I must be later than planned. My watch is in my tennis bag. Mind if I run on? I have to get some dry clothes as well.'

'Of course not, but come around and eat some with us. Maybe tomorrow evening? I'll be here not long after church, but later there'll be a shellfish feast—around five o'clock. I'm staying at 21 Orchard Close; in the village. I'm sure Aunty Gertie and Uncle Charles won't mind.'

'Do check with them first. I'll see you around, matey,' she gives him a peck on the cheek and sets off up to the cliff path.

Once she has gone, he clambers onto a high boulder, feeling a gentle breeze quickly drying his damp body. In the sky, he can see long wispy clouds speeding across from the west indicating that less settled weather might be ahead. He turns and feels the warmth of the sun on his back and legs which radiates a comforting aura of freedom. He longs for this to become a way of life, yet in the back of his mind, he knows he has to return to his home town and school. There he will be under the gaze of unfriendly eyes from all angles, watching his every move and scrutinising everything he does, from his maths homework to his puny efforts on the rugby pitch.

Determined to suppress these unwelcome thoughts, he stares out to sea. The sun is now starting to cast shadows across the shelving rocks creating many areas of darkness amongst the seaweed dangling into the deep fissures. Now even more he can see how the area became known as Blackledge, and although sinister shapes are becoming prominent, he smiles as he thinks of his happy times on these rocks in the last few days.

The last waves now surge over the wreck and he begins to imagine what is happening deep below where the huge eel Jack, the elegant deep-blue Matilda and all the other creatures now roam freely in their element of the open sea. As the waves begin to tumble into the pools in front of him, he realises that soon the whole expanse of rocks will be covered.

Somewhat reluctantly, he changes into his dry shirt and shorts. Slowly, he makes his way up the cliff, frequently looking back to marvel at the great open space of the flooding sea before him, knowing that more than anything else he wants to spend his time exploring the secrets that might be hidden below the tide.

Limpets

Chapter Five

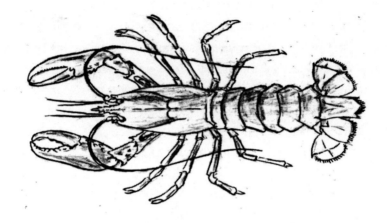

Cow (Hen) Lobster

Discovering the Wild

Early the next morning, Jason marvels at the fine lobster in the fridge, admiring its size and bright orange shell. The evening before, he stood alongside the large pot of simmering salty water as Aunty Gertie plunged it to its death, while assuring Jason this was the quickest and most humane way. He had felt great sadness but was soon transfixed in wonder as it had turned from a rich dark blue to the vibrant orange red. He had already seen it happen with the prawns, but with the lobster the colour transformation was far more dramatic and had held his concentration for many minutes.

Soon, they are all at the Sunday breakfast table. Jason is dressed in his shorts and tee shirt, the clothes he wears for the beach. His face is alert and full of anticipation.

'I do hope, darling, you are not even thinking of going to church like that?' Gertie quizzes. Jason smiles and shakes his head. 'I'm so glad—I don't think the canon would approve! I was brought up to be immaculate for church every Sunday without fail. Mother made sure of that. Sunday was just for church, then lunch and afternoon tea with family. It was a true day of rest.'

Jason gets up from the table. 'Just going to see Old Joe, I'll only be a few minutes. Ready at ten-thirty without fail, promise!' he says as he scurries to the front door. He canters up the road but slows down when there is no sign of Joe on his usual perch at the end of the wall. Slightly perplexed, he turns and slowly walks home to change to his Sunday best.

In a few minutes, he is sitting in the front parlour on a high straight-backed chair. His grey jacket and neat well-pressed matching short trousers reveal his lightly tanned knees above his light-grey gartered socks. His black shoes shine brightly, his school tie is firmly tied with a slim knot, his cap is neatly folded on the table, and his short wavy brown hair is smartly brushed.

Aunty and Uncle are both reading newspapers and say little until they set off for the Church of St David, a little way from the village square. Once it was in the open fields but now it is surrounded by cottages and the graveyard. Many people are outside, talking in the last of the sunshine as a sharp breeze springs from the west.

Inside, the congregation assembles as Jason follows his uncle and aunt to his pew. He marvels at the stained-glass windows, several of which have scenes of boats at sea, some in turbulent weather. Many small models of vessels from yesteryear hang from the vaulted ceiling.

Jason marks the pages of the hymns with small pieces of cardboard and smiles, as he knows all of the service for Palm Sunday. As the organ strikes the notes of the first hymn and the choir leads the congregation into voice, Jason bursts forth as he always does at services.

For three years, he sang in his own parish choir before going to secondary school. His well-tutored soprano tones are noted, even causing the blonde-haired head choirboy to stare over the rows for whoever is singing in such beautiful harmony. In the second hymn, on the last verse, the choir sings a descant. Jason, without thinking, elevates his notes in line with the choir.

Several people turn around and give quizzical stares. One is a large lady, dressed in grey, with a shock of fading red hair over a large white face, with bulbous eyes. She holds strange spectacles close to her eyes,

76

then glares over them as she turns as if to challenge the confidence of the boy soprano.

Unnerved, Jason looks away to ignore her and carries on singing as he is enjoying himself in the full vocal spirit of the service. He sings with equal gusto until the end of the service, when he puts on a more sombre air as everyone files from the church. He and all of the children receive the traditional gift of the raffia palms made into the shape of a cross. Suddenly, he notices Old Joe being assisted by two middle-aged men as he shuffles out on his two sticks. He is wearing a smart-dark green corduroy jacket and a checked tweed tie, which is quite different from his usual attire.

Many people mingle and chatter outside. Charles and Gertie present Jason proudly to several of their friends, all of whom compliment him on his singing, at which he both blushes and smiles. Yet he cannot miss several unwelcome stares from the stern-looking lady and these make their mark in the back of his mind. Suddenly, he sees Abby jostling past a group of people; clearly she is heading for him.

'Hey there, chirpy one!' she blurts out, 'I would love to come to tea; be nice to gobble some prawns!'

Jason looks a touch embarrassed. 'Oh Aunty Gertie, Uncle Charles, this is Abby. We met out crabbing. I meant to ask if she can come and eat some prawns with us as she helped by emptying the net for me. She's from Australia…is that all right?'

Gertie glances at Charles who nods genially. 'Yes, of course. Come for high tea and enjoy some of Jason's catch.'

'Could that be about five,' Jason asks hopefully, 'when I get back from the rocks?'

'I'm afraid it'll be raining before we know it. You probably won't be going anywhere today. And maybe not for a few days if this weather pattern sets in,' Gertie responds. 'But five will be fine,' she smiles charmingly at Abby. 'We shall see you then.'

'Thank you very much,' says Abby then moves away.

Jason gives her a gentle smile, but he is taken back by Gertie's prediction. He knows he has to go to the Blackledge today because it could be the last tide to reveal the secret hole, and he wants to give Jack the conger and Matilda the lobster some more limpets to eat. He looks

77

at the sky sternly as though trying to stop the clouds from raining. As the three of them leave the church grounds, he sees Joe sitting on a wooden bench just outside the porch gate.

'I'd like to speak to him for a moment,' he says.

'Of course,' answers Gertie.

He goes over and calls gently, 'Hello, Mr Joe, it's Jason. Did you eat the crab I prepared for you yesterday?'

The blank dazed face suddenly lights up. 'Ohhh...' Joe sighs loudly, 'the best supper I've had in a long time. Crab, a sweet cow crab, it was so beautiful I couldn't stop eating. Thank ya, thank ya, laddie.'

Jason looks radiant. 'I went back to that hole and sure enough there was both a huge conger and a big lobster, sharing the same hole, just as you said. But I left both of them alone; I wouldn't catch them, or even try.'

'Ha, the old conger likes sharing, cos when she changes shell he'll eat her, ha! Old bully!' Joe says gruffly.

'No! That would be awful! I'll have a llook again today. Poor Matilda,' he whispers under his breath.

'Won't see hole again for few months. Be raining soon, and will carry on for two days or more. Can smell it in th' air. Sea'll be rough. Good for bass fishing though!' the old man says in his weak but knowledgeable voice. Then a rather tarnished black Ford car arrives to take him home. One of the men gets out and assists Joe, and he is gone before Jason can tell him about the lobster he caught.

It is just starting to rain as they arrive back at the house. Jason goes upstairs and changes into his tee shirt and shorts then pushes his nose to the window. Already, the sea in the bay is fading behind a grey screen of steady rain, shrouding any view. It's the first rain since he arrived and he feels cheated that the planned day has gone astray. He is very downcast, then his imagination takes him to the rocks and he can see Jack the conger readily accepting his offerings. He is convinced the conger is reacting to him as he holds a plump mollusc by the finger tips and the creature takes it with surprising gentleness. He sees Matilda snapping the offerings with her sharp slicer claw, cutting each into convenient small pieces to devour quickly. He lies on his back on the bed and stares.

Suddenly, he is interrupted by a tap on the door. 'A bowl of soup on the table, Jason,' comes Gertie's voice, and he glances at his clock and realises his planned outing to the rocks is definitely off, as the tide will be flooding in an hour. The rain is now tumbling persistently and the wind whistles in squalls, tearing the young spring leaves from trees.

Soon all three are sitting at the table, having a warming soup.

'Does that feel better, something warm inside? Don't be too disappointed Jason,' Gertie says sympathetically. 'Now you see how changeable the weather can be!'

'Thank you, Aunty. It's just that today would be the last time I could get to the best holes—all the ones Joe has told me where to find. The next tides are not so big. But it now looks horrible outside!'

'Well, don't forget, we have that lovely lobster to eat, and plenty of crabs!' Charles says, rubbing his hands.

When lunch is over, Jason goes upstairs and spends an hour in his room reading his *Pocket Guide to the Seashore*, making many sketches in pencil in the margins, noting where he found a wide number of species of small creatures and varieties of seaweeds.

Then Gertie calls up the stairs to ask if he would like to prepare the crabs with her, and he goes down to the kitchen, where he enjoys neatly arranging the extracted meat into the large carapaces. He puts a mound of prawns on a large round plate, placing them artistically in concentric rings with a trio of the largest ones crowning the centre.

Gertie brings a jar from the pantry. 'Look, a treat for you. Mayonnaise. It's the really special stuff, much nicer than salad cream. It's the first time I have bought this since rationing finished three years ago. The problem is that we have forgotten many of the better things that weren't available for years. When I saw this in the Home and Colonial, I just had to buy it. I thought, with all this lovely fresh shellfish, we should have the best.'

She places the open jar on the table indicating for Jason to try some. He dips in a spoon and tries it, then scoops some juice and bits of dark crab meat from the tray and tastes it with a little of the creamy white sauce. His face lights up in approval. He then looks at the residual juices from the shells, tastes a drop with a spoon, nods, then carefully pours all of it into a small bowl. He adds a little mayonnaise and all the smaller particles of meat that he thought would otherwise be discarded.

'Just taste this. It'll be lovely with some brown bread!' he says as he places it carefully on the serving platter for the crab.

'You're quite a gourmet, aren't you Jason?' Aunty says with a smile as she sets the plates aside to await their guest. She has also prepared a bowl of cucumber and tomatoes, both thinly sliced and drenched with a little vinegar and pepper; a large plate of sliced wholemeal bread with a chunk of farmhouse salted butter in the centre, and an oval dish of trifle topped with whipped cream. Jason smiles in anticipation.

The rain is easing a little when Abby arrives. She takes off her plastic mac and hangs it on a hook by the door and shakes her blonde hair. Her tanned face and beaming blue eyes have a radiance that puts Aunty and Uncle at ease. As they tuck into the food, she keeps them enthralled with tales of "yabbie-digging" back home and the parties that frequently ensued while they devoured the delicacies. Though she is only two years older than Jason, her confidence and physical development are quite different from his shy demeanour and slightly diminutive body.

Enlivened by her vibrant personality, the high tea is relaxed and convivial. The elders are pleasantly surprised and retire to the sitting room, leaving the Jason and Abby to chat.

'You seem to have a very sociable time in school and lots of fun with your mates,' he suggests, wanting to hear more of her tales.

'Sure, after a year in high school, I knew I must be my own person and tell others what I think. Any big blokes soon took note. But are you the smallest in the class, or nearly?' she probes.

He blushes slightly. 'Well, not quite, a few are smaller. But there are lots of taller boys and most are stronger! The rugby team in particular. I don't play. Only when I'm forced to.'

'Too rough for Jason, eh? Best for rugger means a tough devil. They're all muscles and hair, not soft and smooth-skinned, ha! Rugger's hardly you, my friend. But you've the best voice I've heard. In the school choir?' she quizzes.

'Well, no.' He stares blankly at the floor.

She is taken back. 'Why the heck not? With a soprano voice like that, you could do all the solos, even lead the choir. Why not?' But instantly, she detects he is closing up. 'Hey, come on, didn't mean to offend. Are there any secrets, give me a hint? Please relax. Talk about it; don't stick head in the sand, like an ostrich. Oh gosh, don't cry, please!' she says, comforting him as she sees him in distress. She puts an arm around his shoulder with a hand on his trembling knee. 'Tell me, it will be better. Share with me, I promise you, please, Jason.'

Slowly, the trembling of his upper lip eases enough to allow him to utter a few hesitant words. 'You're right, I was the best at solos and sang in the last concert in junior school. Two of us were competing to do it, and I won. The other boy didn't seem to care. He was always nice to me, but perhaps he was actually envious. Later, we went on to grammar school. I was going to join the school choir and went to the first practice. But a few days later, in the morning break, I went for a walk to where some of the older boys smoked, in a small coppice just off the playing fields. This particular day it seemed nobody was there. Then I saw a tall angry boy following me. It was the other boy's elder brother, who was in the fifth form. He called me horrid things, saying my voice was awful, like a baby's. Then he punched me twice in the throat. I couldn't speak, or even cry it was so painful. Right here,' he taps his throat near his Adam's apple. 'Then he did it again in my stomach and jumbo-kicked me on the thigh so I couldn't move, and told me to give up singing before he finished me for good. Some days, I still see him and dare not look at him at all.'

Jason trembles as he relates the story, and Abby looks at him in amazement.

'Gee, watta bully. Did you report him, tell any of the teachers? Obviously needs to be sorted—the bully!' she says in shock at his distress.

'They'd only call me puny, cos I don't want to play rugby, go to the gymnasium and do all the rough training that the bigger boys take pride in. Lifting weights and all that. It's not me, I know. I go swimming as I can do that alone, and I'm quite good at it as well. I'm certainly not afraid of the water, you've seen that.' He sighs heavily. 'But no, you are the first person I've told. Not even my parents know. They would make a fuss and that's no good for me when I'm alone and meet that terrible boy.' He begins to compose himself. 'Still, no one else in the school has caught a lobster, crabs, prawns, a conger. Nobody!'

'And none of them will have had the fab tea we just did, and you're right, they couldn't catch the stuff you can. Good on you, stick to it. Just ignore them,' she says.

'Yes, thanks, but it's difficult to ignore them when I see them almost every day. I dread going back to that school.' Then he rallies a little. 'What's your school like? Do you like it?'

'Well, yes I do. But I'm in a small private school with only a hundred or so pupils, about twelve in a class, so we know each other well. And we have to do everything together. Sure there are rows, but it's quickly sorted out, usually settled in the dormitory.'

'You mean you sleep there?' Jason cuts in. 'That's posh!' After a slight hesitation he says, 'What does your father do? If you don't mind me asking.'

'Of course not, he's in the High Commission in London; that's why I'm here. They both travel a lot, mainly around the country but also back home. So it's easier for me to be in boarding school here. In the hols, I stay with a cousin here if my parents are away. Dad's fanatical about tennis, as we have some great players back home,' she clenches her fist and holds it high. 'And your dad, what's he about? If you don't mind me asking, that is.'

'Well, he's a manager in a steel works in the Midlands. He worked for the same company here when young, long ago. He moved so that he could progress to eventually be a manager in a new plant, a far better job prospect.'

'And do they have any hobbies or sports?' she digs further.

'He goes off walking the moors, dales, mountains, to anywhere. Usually, my mother goes as well, and so do I. Some of the places are particularly pretty, particularly the lakes, but it can be boring. The best times are when we do some rock climbing. He has drummed in all the safety precautions to take, so I am pretty confident about simple climbing, as I do on the rocks and going up and down parts of the cliff where it's safe and easy. But at the end of the day too often I end up sitting outside a pub while they talk to people inside. And that's boring, and why I read so much, and discovered books on the seashore. I have quite a collection now!'

'Do you have any brothers or sisters?' Abby asks.

Jason shakes his head, 'No, It's just me.'

'Huh, me neither,' she shrugs her shoulders.

Suddenly, they both jump at a loud muffled bang from the back yard. There is a triumphant cry from Uncle Charles. They look at one another and quickly go outside. It has stopped raining. A big air rifle is propped against a chair in the yard. Uncle is marching up the garden. He bends down amongst some cabbages and pulls up a black and white bird with a long black tail.

'A magpie!' Abby calls to him. 'You shot it?'

'Ha, yes! One clean shot and dropped it. Can ye hear the other one calling, that rasping noise? They're after the blackbird's nest in that shrub!' he points at it for emphasis. 'I'll wait for the other to come looking for his mate. They're the bullies of the bird world here. Ruined all the nests last year. Take the eggs, or the young birds from the nest, whether song thrushes, pigeons, hedge-sparrows, robins, anything. Nasty things! So I bought the air rifle. A powerful rifle; they won't get them this year!'

He ties the dead bird by the neck and hangs it from a pole to ward off others.

'A warning to bullies!' he says smugly and sits down, clutching the rifle to await the appearance of the magpie's mate, which is squawking in some trees a short distance away. Then he stands again and calls to Jason and Abby. 'Hey, ye didn't say about the oyster! Found it amongst seaweed as I cleaned out your bag. Note that!' he says looking knowingly at Abby. 'I was the one who cleaned his bag out. Not him. He was so excited by the lobster, he forgot the oyster.'

Jason picks up immediately. 'Oh, yes, I found it in a pool at Blackledge. I could see it was alive.'

'Aye, come on then, I'll open it so we can have a taste,' Uncle says. 'Come, I'll show ye a local trick!'

He pulls the flat-shelled mollusc from under a mound of seaweed in the corner of the yard then rinses it under the outside tap. Then they both follow him into the kitchen and scullery where the iron range glows with hot coals. He pushes the oyster between the horizontal cast-iron slats at the front of the fire.

'The old oysterman's trick. These are hard to open!' he says in a hushed tone, 'but in a few secs, ye'll taste the sea. Don't cook oysters, the flavour is spoiled, but this will just warm it enough for it to gape, and then you have to catch all the juice; and as for the taste, mmm.'

With a cloth in his hand, he wriggles the mollusc from the fire and places it on a plate. As juice oozes from it, he slips a knife between the two shells and gently prises off the top one. This reveals a creamy plump blob of soft flesh with a frill like a comb around the edge. He takes it to the kitchen table and picks up a couple of slices of bread.

'Now dip ye bread into the juice.' He shakes a little pepper and a few drops of vinegar over the oyster.

'Gee, see what you mean! We've oysters back home, but not like these. Ours are longer and have crinkly shells. They taste good, but man, this is special! What a flavour, eh, Jason?' Abby says with delight, as Jason picks up a cube of the soggy bread and gobbles it in one.

'Now just a tiny taste of meat,' Uncle says. 'I'll cut it into slivers, ye'll just get a taster. Could do with six each of these!' he adds with a laugh.

'So could I!' Abby replies, and they reverently taste the tiny morsels with many "Ohs" and "Ahs" as they savour the delicacy.

'The taste is amazing!' Jason exclaims. 'It's not salty or fishy, just sweet and strangely creamy, and very iron-y; that's the taste it leaves behind. I'll have to keep an eye out for more.'

'Ya won't find many; used to be thousands, even millions here, and lots of boats fishing them. But the landings fell off and all ye boats moved away or rotted on their moorings. When I was a boy, yes, I remember the last few boats, and the rough old devils who worked them.' Charles nods and smiles at them both. 'Wonderful to taste it again—but more please, Jason! Now, I must go an' shoot that other flippin' magpie!' And he steps out into the garden once more.

Jason and Abby go back into the parlour and she gathers her coat to depart. Noticing that his expression is suddenly a little serious, Abby says, 'What are you thinking about?'

'Joe said that congers are the bullies of the coastline,' he says tentatively.

'Well, guess they are. In Oz, we've moray eels; they're really vicious, certainly bullies. Eat anything that dares to come near. And I bet Jack the conger will eat anything. Even Matilda, given half a chance,' she laughs ruefully.

'Don't say that. I believe he's very gentle, and shares his food with her. I think they live very happily together. He's a nice eel, not a bully. I like Jack and he likes me to feed him limpets. He's friendly. I just hope those bully boys don't find the secret hole, or they'll yank him out with their big barbed gaff. Nasty boys!' he utters this with feeling and she smiles.

'As long as they leave Matilda alone, that's what I care about. She is the most beautiful blue I have ever seen.'

'But Joe said it'll be months before the secret hole is revealed again, not until the autumn spring tides, and only if there isn't any wind blowing,' he sighs. 'So maybe they will be safe.'

'Yup, imagine they'll be in a tranquil garden under the waves for all that time. Lucky things,' she says cheerfully. 'Well, time to go.' She looks at Jason as he escorts her to the front gate, and after giving him a little peck on the cheek she skips happily down the road.

Later in the evening, Jason goes to his room to read before bed and gazes out of the window across the bay. The sky is now clear and stars begin to twinkle over the water to the distant dark elusive horizon. He crawls into bed and, staring up at the ceiling, he imagines the sea garden that Abby described—the swirling of the currents in the long horse-tail weed brings distorted images of crabs, lobsters and his friend Jack the eel as they twirl around in the imaginary sea above him. Soon, he is in a deep relaxing sleep, dreaming of the multitude of wonderful seashore creatures.

Native Oyster

Chapter Six

Bull (Cock) Crab

Challenges Beneath

The twice-daily ebb and flow of the tides wash the shores and rocky outcrops of the coastline, revealing the expanses of estuary, sandy bays and craggy headlands on an eternal, unrelenting cycle. Yet, for many weeks and months, none of the ebb tides has uncovered the lowest rocks and Jason's secret hole where the conger and lobster reside remains hidden in the tranquil depths. The sea life on this part of the coast carries on in its ever-watery way. The highest spring tides are not destined to return until late August, approaching the autumn equinox.

The lazy summer neap tides and the fortnightly spring tides do not uncover the lowest rocks. The area surrounding the wreck is permanently submerged. This makes the feeding opportunities for all creatures far greater, but during the brighter long hours of the days as summer approaches, many of the predators prefer to rest, hunting only by night.

Jack the conger stays in his lair through the day, taking in the scents of possible prey that he can pursue when night falls. Matilda the lobster rests in safety far back in the darkness of the hole where the sunlight will never reach. Her twitching feelers sense every movement and scent that drifts by and convey images to her central nerve that runs from the proboscis to the tip of her tail. A fine row of tail hairs detects anything that might approach from behind.

She stands on the tips of her eight legs, elevating her body high from the muddy floor. Her tail is splayed fully so she can gently fan fresh water over her treasure of thousands of tiny eggs festooned between the pairs of tiny paddles under her extended tail. She has done this continually for many months while her brood develops, turning the raven-black eggs to pale pink as gradually the tiny lobsters within them begin to take on their form.

Nightly, Jack goes in pursuit of food. While out hunting, he scoops up anything that looks tasty, but his last prey, he brings back to his lair to devour. Frequently, he might crunch a crustacean or dead fish, creating much detritus of mature morsels for Matilda and the host of rock prawns that also inhabit the hole. These jolly little creatures keep the floor clean, and, they always escape the greedy gulp of Jack's jaws, or a snap from the lobster's agile claws.

The scent which Jack picks up as the days of summer lengthen is the bounty of the best succulence in their garden. It is the time when all crabs—and every other crustacean—go through the regular growing routine of casting their shells, and the sea garden floor is littered with empty cases. Some creatures lose a leg or claw during this process. Others might die and become food for numerous fish and indeed other crustaceans. But the real prize for the scavengers and predators is the jelly-soft shell of the newly exposed crabs. Many creatures want a feast of these.

In this season of plenty, there are also numerous small green shore crabs, and their larger cousins the orange belly, invading the rocks from the deeper water. Additional visitors, who emerge as if by magic from the ocean, are the deep-brown velvet swimming crabs. The back shell of large ones only measures about three inches, but they have frightening red eyes and slashing angry pinchers. Jack finds these particularly tasty but they are more difficult to catch because their swimming rear legs and overall agility usually carry them to safety.

An easier catch for Jack is the edible brown cow crab. Now many are jelly soft after casting their shells in readiness for breeding. At this point, the males are protecting their mates, tucking them between their legs and tail in a manoeuvre that also facilitates the fertilisation of the eggs inside the females.

On his nightly feeding foray, Jack will scoop up pairs of smaller green crabs in one, enjoying the crunch of the tougher shell of the male and the wobbly succulence of the female in one mouthful. But he is as greedy as the walrus and the carpenter eating oysters on the briny beach. He wants the ones of largest size, and seeks out the biggest soft brown crabs. The males sit resolutely on their partners, and it takes a sudden and unexpected attack to catch a bull off his guard. But for Jack, the prize is worth the time-consuming effort.

It is a moonless summer night and the sea is like a mill pond. The rocks are now teeming with life and Jack picks up a scent he knows so well. Close by, within fifty yards, a large crab is going through the process of casting. He glides elegantly across the rocks hugging the undulations with his long, powerful tail. It is made more impressive by the strong fins that propel him effortlessly.

Within a deep scoop on the side of a narrow cleft, Jack detects a large bull crab where the serrated wrack swashes gently in the water as it reaches for the sunlight. On a low tide, this settles over the lair, covering its residents. In the cranny below, the empty shell of the newly cast cow is a perfect replica of her, yet is lifeless and hollow. Her new body, soft and vulnerable, is safely tucked under the bull whose great black-tipped claws are splayed widely as a warning to any unwanted visitors.

Jack wants this large delectable mouthful for his supper and he is determined to get it. The bull is over six inches across the carapace and the soft cow is smaller— her empty shell is barely four inches. Jack, hugging the rock with his muscular body, inches closer to make a surprise attack from above, but the bull crab is securely anchored to the pitted limestone rock with his eight-pointed legs. His powerful legs and massive claws wedge his body firmly over the cow.

Suddenly, Jack makes a lunge at the crab, his splayed tail propelling him like a javelin, hitting the bull full on. The bull crab is called Trevor. He sticks resolutely to his position. Just like a barnacle, he refuses to be dislodged a fraction of an inch. He tenses every one of his legs, hanging on as a spider would to its web, locking his body resolutely.

The powerful conger—who is over six feet long and weighs in excess of fifty pounds—knows that if he persists, eventually, the crab will weaken and separate from its mate. He bashes the shell repeatedly with his great head and strong bony jaw. But he is unsuccessful, and so he opens his jaws revealing the hard ridges of sandpaper-like cartilage. Then he gapes fully and raises his rows of needle-like teeth. He aims to grip the back of the shell to heave the crab out of its stronghold.

Trevor however, a stubborn creature, is as obstinate as a cricketer who refuses to leave his crease whatever the bowler hurls at him. Three more poundings make the bull shift slightly, leaving one claw exposed; now Trevor is waiting to nip the intruder with his powerful claw. The conger tries to grip the corner of Trevor's carapace, but the crab closes its claw on Jack's lower jaw bone, and he hangs on firmly.

Latched securely onto his victim in this way, he will not release his grip, and the conger is trapped. Though Jack tries to pull himself away, he is locked onto the crab, and even with his great weight and a vigorous twisting of the body, he cannot set himself free. The wound inflicted by the crab bleeds profusely, attracting many prawns and small rock fish—blennies, gobies and bullheads—to investigate the scent.

Now, as his temper flares like that of a shark in a feeding frenzy, Jack contorts his body like a coil in an attempt to heave himself free. The obstinate Trevor firms his claw, crunching further into the bony jaw. Soon, it crumbles under such continual pressure. The two parts of the hefty claw pass through the cartilage and the tips of his pinchers come together, taking a slab of skin from the jaw. With its severed lower jaw, the conger is now suddenly able to squirm free from the crab's relentless grip. The wound oozes lots of blood and Jack has not won the anticipated meal.

Angered and injured, he swims vigorously away into the open sea, finally coming to rest way beyond the submerged wreck. Shocked and disorientated by his tussle, he propels himself over the undulating sea bed in search of prey, but the power of his jaws has gone and he can only suck in several small crabs that try in vain to hide. He will not tackle a large bull crab for a while. He returns to his cave to skulk close to Matilda, who sits patiently waiting for the eggs she is carrying to hatch.

Such is the abundance of moulting smaller green and fiddler crabs that many hide in any cover they can find, as not all have protective mates. These are easy prey for Jack, even in his wounded state, but it takes several dozen to fill his stomach. And there is a lot of competition for them. Bass with their gaping powerful mouths will swallow a large crab or anything they come across. Soles and topknots hug the rocks with their flexible spring-like bodies searching for small crustaceans and molluscs and no shell is too tough for them.

The pretty multi-coloured ballan and corkwing wrasse that can grow to about ten inches long have powerful small mouths. They harvest tufts of seaweed to make their sponge-like nests that are wedged in clefts in the rocks where they can lay eggs to nurture over the summer. They are adept at prising small limpets, barnacles and mussels from the rocks, and any small crustaceans. Like their warm-water cousins of the coral reefs, they will scour the jagged rocks where hunting is more difficult for bass, whiting and pollack, which will search for easier prey elsewhere.

Dog fish, huss and tope, related to the mighty sharks of the oceans, scavenge the rocks for anything dead or alive. They scoop up any crab vulnerable during the moulting season, and although not the size of Jack, they are competition for food. And as well as being prey to all kinds of fish, crabs are vulnerable to their own kind. All types of crabs will wait for their own or other juveniles to cast shells, and these youngsters become the food for the larger ones. It is a garden of eating and be eaten, so everything is on its guard.

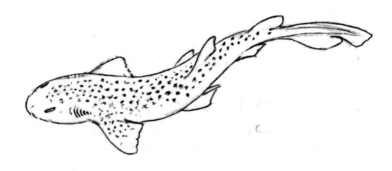

Dogfish or Huss

After his debilitating encounter, Jack rests in his hole and bides his time for something large and succulent to pass, as for a while, he is unable to hunt effectively. After many days of lying quietly, the cartilage on his broken jaw is reforming into a tough ridge that allows him to flex his jaws once again, and he senses nature's healing process will soon enable him to go hunting. Then he is ready. Slowly and stealthily, the large conger emerges from his dark cave and swims along the shell-strewn sea bed seeking sustenance.

The arrival of a swarm of spindle-legged spider crabs will be welcome, for they also come to this rocky patch to cast their shells. The bright orange-brown crustaceans are easy to spot and make a very satisfying mouthful, but only when soft, as normally their shells are very spiny and unyielding.

As soon as they discard their armour, they plant a garden of small seaweed on their carapaces to confuse potential predators, such as Jack. They sit silent and still for many days, perhaps several weeks, as nature takes its course hardening their shells. Any movement would be detected by the many fish that scour the sea bed for fertile pickings.

The invading spider crabs are voracious feeders. They move like an army on their seasonal migration, and will devour every edible morsel, including smaller crabs. When they arrive, most other creatures move elsewhere to feed. At the same time, the horse tail, also called oar weed, grows in the sunshine, photosynthesising rapidly to become several feet long. This makes great camouflage for crustaceans and many of the spider crabs cling to the basal stumps of the horse tail while the fronds above sway gently in the tide. Most are ready to moult.

Jack finds himself in an area that is barren but for the spider crabs. He nestles amongst some of the many oar weed branches that have broken away and fallen to the sea floor. Around him are numerous cast spider-crab shells. He waits curled in the weed for something edible to emerge. He knows many of these crabs will shed their shells, but finding them is more difficult. They lie in crevices and corners, and amongst the mounds of dead seaweed, out of sight.

All crustaceans go through the process of ecdysis. For many species, the moulting is a fairly quick experience, but for lobsters and brown crabs their hefty claws, particularly those of a bull, prolong the process. It can be a difficult time before the new shell is eventually set free from the old, as the huge bulk of the claw has to pass through the minuscule connecting joint that carries signals of movement back to the central nerve.

Large lobsters often take many hours to shed so they head to the protective refuge of a dark cranny or deep hole where they can be relatively safe away from scavengers. As with crabs, the emerging body is an exact replica of the original, but is considerably larger. Every part is renewed, including the stomach, gills, sinews, intestine. It is one of the true wonders of nature.

The spider crab with its bulky body that can grow to the size of a large saucer and spindly four-jointed legs can go through moulting more easily and it can scurry away to refuge. Jack sits and waits, aware that many large bass are cruising above him in search of the same fodder. Bass survey their territory from above either in shoals or individually. Adroit and powerful, their speed means they have fewer predators and hence are efficient hunters, diving at lightning speed onto any possible meal, whether other fish, crustaceans or carrion. Jack's perspective is far more limited so he has to sit for his opportunity to rise and present itself.

Motionless, he is poised, and waits, all the time getting more and more hungry. He knows that Trevor the bull crab taught him a salutary lesson and now he must not take chances. But as more and more spider crabs crowd the area, he also knows it will not be long before he has a satisfying feed. He waits for one of them to cast its shell in isolation where he can grab the prize before other hungry fish descend. But Jack is a great age, possibly over forty years old, and has survived many lean times in the past and he is prepared to sit and wait for the next easy meal to arrive. It could be a fiddler crab that has cast shell without a protective mate; a juvenile crab that has no safe cover; a green or a yellow belly shore crab. An unsuspecting blennie or gobie can be scooped in a quick gulp. All are welcome nourishment for Jack. He will not go hungry.

Barnacles

Chapter Seven

Corkwing Wrasse

Probing the Depths

On Easter Sunday, the sky is overcast and there is a gentle westerly breeze following days of cooler northerly winds. When unable to explore the shore, Jason has spent much time in the village library looking at many books on seashore life. One day, he took the tram to the large town further along the bay to visit its Museum which is close to the terminus. He was fascinated by the exhibits of relics from ancient Egypt, and also the cases of many different stuffed birds. But he spent most of his time gathering information on the sea shore, particularly the history of fishing in the area.

Amongst the historical publications, he found a small book entitled *An Eye Witness Account of Shipwrecks on the Roweg Coast* by Eynon Johns. He read through it in little over an hour and was riveted by the descriptions of the storms and the frantic efforts to rescue many from drowning. He noted particularly the account of the Stenvetia that wrecked off the Blackledge Rocks in 1918.

'The MV Stenvetia, having been damaged by enemy action towards the end of the War, was on tow to the scrapyard on the River Nythern. Just ten knots from its destination on the afternoon of September 5th the weather turned and a full gale blew from the sou'west. Both the coaster and tug were driven close to the rocks off Blackpond Bay. The wind changed to the west and then the nor'west, pushing her sou'east, and causing the vessel to founder off Blackledge, just as the full ebb was approaching. The tow ropes parted and the tug managed to fight through the pounding seas to the safety of deeper water. The 900-ton iron ship was battered by heavy seas and began to break up as the tide rose, when the stern section parted from the hull. The buoyant bow superstructure eventually wrecked onto the rocks on the east of Longbeach. After many months, it was cut up and salvaged. The stern remains wedged in the rocks off Blackledge to this day. It is visible daily at low tide. On lowest spring tides, it can be reached by crossing the rocks on foot.'

Jason copied the exact words into his notebook and reads them again as he considers his next trip to the rocks. But there is still his schoolwork. Although he has written a second letter to his parents, praising his hosts and eulogising about the meals, he has not opened his satchel or started his homework. He has not seen Joe for several days as the frequent showers have prevented the old man from getting out.

Jason is prepared for church early and walks there with Charles and Gertie. Many people are gathering outside St David's Church half an hour before the Eucharist at eleven. Everyone is in their best attire with suits pressed and shoes burnished to a bright shine. Jason stands with Gertie and Charles, exchanging good wishes with all who pass. Suddenly, the ginger-haired lady appears at the churchyard gate. She speaks briefly to other people then strides past Jason and nods to Charles and Gertie, but then turns to Jason to deliver a sudden penetrating glance. Then they file with everyone else into the nave and take their seats on the solid, hard pine chairs, and he tries to put it out of his mind.

Jason keeps glancing back to the door awaiting some familiar faces. He sees Nicholas and Roger, the brothers he met briefly on the rocks when he caught the conger, and they smile and wave discreetly. After a minute or so, Joe arrives at the door, assisted by the usual two men, and he shuffles to his regular seat towards the front. Then Abby enters, but she is talking to two slightly older girls and doesn't see Jason's expectant face.

By now, the organist is in full stride, playing seasonal music that is very familiar to Jason. Enthused by this, he relaxes then hums along to himself, his eyes fixed on the model boats that hang as mobiles in front of each of the aisle windows of the nave.

Once everyone is seated, the choir files in, singing an Easter anthem in full voice. Although eager to join in the singing, this time Jason restrains himself, nervous about unwanted attention. The preacher welcomes his congregation, then the magnificence of the service commences with "There is a Green Hill Far Away" that everyone knows, and the singing volume soars.

Jason breathes deeply, awaiting the key notes from the choir, then, despite his concerns, bursts forth, hymning with all his heart and soul, not looking either side but straight towards the elevated cross in the crossing of the beautiful cruciform church. In full voice and positively radiant as he gives all into the hymn, he is nevertheless conscious that he is drawing the attention of some other members of the congregation.

As he sings the final Amen, he lowers his eyes and becomes aware of the powerful gaze from the ginger-haired lady, who once more turns around, and her whole face seems to convey disapproval as it did a week earlier. He tries to ignore her as the congregation sits for the reading, then kneels for prayers.

He knows every word of the Eucharist and is tempted to sing the canticles with the choir, but his caution takes over and he remains quiet. He saves himself for the remaining three hymns, deliberately avoiding any possible eye contact with anyone. There is a long queue for Communion and he stands with perfect posture, although he is the smallest person to take the bread and wine. He was confirmed just a few weeks earlier in his home parish church, and this is now his second time to take Communion away from there. Again, he holds his poise impeccably and returns to his pew to pray.

Soon, the service comes to an end, and with the organ playing a triumphant anthem, the congregation files outside where Jason hopes to meet two people before they depart.

Aunty Gertie pats Jason on the shoulder. 'Well, your lovely voice was certainly noticed, and appreciated, Jason!' She doesn't mention the look from the ginger-haired lady.

'Ye could be quite a show-stopper, lad. I'm sure the choir heard you, enchanting!' Charles adds.

Jason smiles, but remembers he has to look for Joe and Abby. 'I must go for a few minutes to catch Joe before his car comes. I'll be back soon!' He weaves his way through the throng searching for Joe.

All the wooden seats that circle the churchyard, where Joe usually sits, are taken. Eventually, he sees him being escorted to the old car that brings him to and from church each Sunday. Disappointed, his eyes then flash around looking for Abby. When he spots her, she is still with the two older girls and he is uncertain whether to approach, fearing he might embarrass her in front of her friends. He takes a small notebook and pencil from his pocket, writes a short message, rips out the page and folds it.

He tries to attract her attention but to no avail, and finally plucks up the courage to approach the three of them. As she spots him, her eyes light up and she waves welcomingly.

'Well, knew you was about, everyone could hear that voice! Beautiful,' she calls in her strong brash way. The others with her are too engaged with each other and ignore Jason, but their lack of grace is compensated for by Abby's exuberant praise. He slips the note to her and says "Today!" under his breath. She looks away, flashes her eyes at the paper and discreetly nods back, and cheerily they part.

Charles, Gertie and Jason walk back along the sea front and feel the cool breeze from the sea. It is approaching high tide and the sluggish flood of the neap tide slowly inches up the sea wall.

'When do the next spring tides start, Jason? I bet ye can't wait to get to the rocks again,' says Charles, looking out across the sea.

'It's not for a few days yet, I'm sure,' Gertie cuts in. 'Besides, I do think Jason you need to do all that homework, for I know you haven't started yet—your satchel is still buckled closed! But that's tomorrow. We have our Easter feast today!'

'What are we having, Aunty?' he enquires keenly.

'A surprise!' she replies. 'You'll see, or smell,' and they walk on.

Arriving back home, Jason immediately comments on the aroma wafting from the kitchen. It's unusual and mild with a savoury sweetness of herbs and an elusive meatiness. Clearly Gertie has prepared an extra special treat.

Half an hour later, after cooking the vegetables and making the gravy, she presents a feast onto the fully-extended dining room table. Three china tureens containing the vegetables and a large sauce boat with a china ladle brimming with pale brown gravy make their appearance. Then she enters once more with a large oval carving dish displaying a huge golden-brown roasted chicken. It is surrounded by crisp roast potatoes and quartered parsnips that are partly caramel brown and creamy yellow from their natural sweetness.

There is a mound of well-cooked stuffing showing chunks of onions and herbs from the garden, set off by the rich green of leafy sage and sausage meat, plus a small covered dish of savoury white bread sauce. She looks pleased with her presentation.

Charles stands. Even he is surprised and says, 'My word, ye've been busy, how magnificent, Gertie dearest!'

He is quickly joined by Jason who claps. 'You said surprise, Aunty, but I have never seen a chicken like that! Everything looks superb.' They cheer in delight as Gertie smiles modestly.

After saying grace, Charles angles the platter towards him and takes a long bone-handled carving knife and matching fork. Carving expertly, he lays slices of the breast on the potatoes and parsnips to keep it warm, then carves some of the meat from the legs and places an assortment of the light meat of the breast and nut-brown leg meat onto the three plates, adding a spoonful of stuffing that has been cooked in the cavity of the bird. The hazel-coloured gravy is pooled onto the side of each plate.

Jason takes a small amount of each vegetable: vibrant green spring cabbage, orange carrots, the sticky parsnips and one crisp brown potato, arranging them neatly on his plate.

'This chicken's delicious!' Jason enthuses. 'It's my favourite of all, but I haven't tasted it since Christmas. This is really wonderful, Aunty—absolutely the best.'

She smiles and Charles nods as he savours each mouthful. 'This is from the marvellous farm on Moorland,' she says. 'They breed these especially for Easter. Sometimes—and this is even more special—we have a Michaelmas goose from there as an autumn treat, and that's the most delicious of all. Maybe we'll have one this year, Charles; it's been a few years since we've bought one. If you're here for half-term Jason, perhaps we could have it then. I'd love you to taste their goose, for you really do seem to enjoy good food, dearest boy!'

'Good idea, Gert, what ya think, Jason? I'll take ya there one day. They're nice people, always do a good job. All their poultry looks happy on the farm and safe out in the fields. No foxes there ya know. Those bullies will kill all the animals just for fun, not for food. But Alf sorts them out. He was a sniper in the war. What a time that was! Poor fellah, five years and never came home until war was over. He said lived on his nerves, hardly slept, cos someone might jump you if you're asleep. But he reckons he sees in the dark, and so can spot foxes. Doesn't want them taking his animals, he cares for them. He somehow brought his sniper's rifle home, with loads of bullets, so if he reckons a fox is about he'll sit up, in the bedroom window, spot them, and bang! That's their lot!' Charles chuckles. 'Nobody messes with Alf. Good for him!'

'Here, here!' Jason joins in the elation. 'Yes, I'd love to see the farm!' But already he is wondering if there might be spring tides at half-term in the autumn, for deep inside he is anxious, wondering if he will be able to visit the rocks again later in the year. Most of all, he does not relish the thought of returning to the Midlands, and even worse, his school.

They continue to eat heartily and everything tastes wonderful to Jason, who has not had vegetables with this intensity of flavour before this visit. Aunty then serves her final surprise for pudding. She presents a large dish with a golden crumble top.

'Ah! I think you'll enjoy this as well,' Charles says beaming. 'Is it apple crumble?' Jason asks.

'Aye, but with a difference. Aunty will explain.'

Gertie comes back into the room with a sauce boat of custard. She smiles. 'Yes, Jason, apple crumble—we pick lots of Bramleys from our friends' orchard. We can have as many of the windfalls as we like. The perfect ones we store and these last up to Christmas, and the rest we cook and seal in Kilner jars, and these last all winter. We also pick blackberries in September and do the same thing, and this is a combination of them both!'

'Well, it's so tasty and unusual—for me, that is. What a fabulous meal. Thank you both so much,' Jason says.

Uncle retires to the parlour once the table is cleared as Jason helps with the washing up. Soon, he is thinking of a short walk to look for Old Joe.

'I'm going to see if Joe is there now as the sun is out, for the next tides start later in the week,' he says to Aunty as they finish drying the plates.

'That's fine, but do take a coat with you, and don't forget, you invited Abby to come here later,' Aunty reminds him.

He changes from his Sunday best into clean sports clothes and marches along the road in hope, but there is no sign of Joe. He sits on the wall where the old man is usually perched, and begins to daydream of the days when Joe was young and well-known as the best local fisherman, who knew every inch of the coastline. His mind then lurches back to his Midlands home, where the sea is seen only on postcards. He remembers a cantankerous school mistress whose tales of the seaside were nothing but candy floss and donkey rides. She was so like the grim-faced woman he has seen in church. He hopes he will not see her again, and feels the same about that school mistress.

He walks down to the sea front, gazes for a while at the sea birds bobbing lazily on the sluggish tide, and then stands to stroll back. But walking towards him is the old trawler man Skipper Jonny wearing his flat cloth cap. He is too close for Jason to avoid.

'Caught anything yet?' he scowls at Jason, who keeps walking.

'Well, actually, yes! Lots of prawns and plenty of crab,' Jason replies confidently, looking back at the man and deciding not to mention the lobster which he wants to remain a secret.

'I bet the crabs weren't big enough! Where did y'catch them?' comes a sharp retort.

'In the sea!' Jason says smartly and grins, then starts to walk on.

'Cheeky little crwt! I'll box your ears for sure. Watch it, kid!' Skipper Jonny shouts pointing a finger at Jason, who turns to look then walks quickly away.

Jason trots up the hill to Joe's vacant wall seat. He sits and stares over the roof tops out to the sea, considering with unease the man's unfriendly comments. Suddenly, his thoughts are interrupted when he spots Abby walking up past the shops towards him. He glances at his watch—quarter to five already! He rushes back home to help to prepare tea, but Aunty already has set the small table impeccably awaiting Abby's arrival.

'Excellent timing, Jason,' Aunty calls from the kitchen. She then appears with a bowl of crabmeat from the ice box of the refrigerator which she puts on the table. 'There! Everything is ready.'

At that second, the door-bell rings. Abby has a short floral dress that personifies spring colours. She is clutching a bunch of daffodils wrapped in newspaper that are for Jason's aunt and a light coat over her arm. Jason takes her into the parlour and Gertie comes in with a tray of tea. She is presented with the daffodils. She is surprised and overcome with the warm gesture from such a young girl and thanks her profusely.

'Beautiful fresh dressed crab, darling, caught by Jason,' she says, uncovering the bowl of flaky white and ochre meat with a blob of mayonnaise in the middle. She brings in a vase for the daffodils and puts them on the sideboard. 'We're having our high tea in the dining room. You darling two enjoy yourselves. If you need any more, please just call.'

'Thank you so much,' says Abby. 'This does look a treat!'

The two tuck into the crab and salads, loading neat mounds onto slices of brown bread. Jason cuts his into bite-sized pieces, and Abby follows his example. She savours each mouthful with relish.

'When are you next going on the rocks, cos this is scrumptious. As good as yabbies, different, creamier, richer but splendid indeed, my friend!' she mutters as she eats away.

'I've never had fresh crab before this holiday,' Jason says. 'Once we had some tinned stuff but although it was quite nice, it was nothing like this. The next lobster I catch, you must share with me. The first I gave to Aunty. She loves them and it's a rare treat for her as Charles rarely went on the rocks. He played rugby, so with all the training there was no time for fishing. Still, he's a very good gardener—I have never tasted such delicious vegetables. Now, the low tides should start on Thursday, but it depends on winds. They are not such big spring tides, so I won't get near the wreck. That's why I want to see Joe for some extra tips on where to look.'

'Will I see you before then, cos term must start soon afterwards, I guess?'

'I've tried not to think of school, even though I do have lots of homework. It's waiting for me upstairs. I really can't bear to think of it, or school. I just wish I could stay here.' he sighs.

'Yes, you told me how much you disliked school. It *is* a shame though. I kinda like school, it's fun.'

'I know you do, but, I hate it. It's not the work, it's the people! And not just some of the boys. A sour-faced woman in church so reminds me of a teacher in the last school. And she was horrible, a cow. No, cows are nice, she was just plain awful,' he realises his words are getting alarmingly strong so he shuts up.

There is a pause in the chatter for a few moments as Jason, looking a tad blank, reflects on the woman and her ominous gaze.

'Come on, matey, get some more of it off your chest. Really, do tell me, it's better to talk about it, believe me!' Abby stares directly at Jason who tries to avoid her gaze, but she prods his tummy. 'Come on!' she insists.

He breathes deeply several times, exuding reluctance. She grabs his hand and stares at him. A tear runs down his face which she sympathetically wipes away.

'All right. Have you got all afternoon?' he says very quietly. 'And all evening as well!' she clutches his quivering hand, bringing a slight smile to his face. 'Tell me about the school teacher, the nasty martinet!'

He sighs. 'She was strict. I was in her class for a year, and she often picked on me. Why, I don't know. I was always in the top five, but she always picked holes in my English, my maths—perhaps for just one tiny mistake—and my singing. The worst time was when she was out of the room with the headmaster. A few boys started larking about and soon most were joining in, eventually including me. She came back and went mad. She lined us all up and we had to say sorry for all the noise. Afterwards, we had to file back past her. Then she slapped me on the face so hard, three times. She didn't touch anyone else, just me and I could see others sniggering. And it really hurt. It was difficult not to cry then, but I certainly did all that night. That was one of many things.' He stops speaking and looks away.

In a gentle voice, Abby says, 'Feel better sharing that? She sounds really unfair and nasty. Good, now she's in the past. Another story?'

'The woman in church, she's just like her. This horrid mistress would come close to me and shout at anything, and, her breath smelt foul, and her body stank of sweat; revolting.'

Abby nods sympathetically.

'But there are other bullies,' Jason continues. 'Too many. The worst was a year ago. We went on a weekend school camping break, I hated it. Most of the boys were bigger than me. One bullying ruffian was bad enough in school, but when he was away, oh, it was awful. Why he picked on me, I don't know. He's two years ahead of me, a first-year boy. He sneered at everything I did in school. Perhaps he was a friend of the lout who punched me for winning the singing competition, don't know. But on the camping weekend…well, where do I start?'

He looks at her and she nods again urging him to continue, opening both hands in a gesture of encouragement.

'I'd made a thumb stick to use when walking or camping. I'd cut it from a blackthorn in January when the wood is rock-hard. I spent many nights whittling it into shape. It was different from the single-V thumb sticks. It was longer with a second grip six inches below the top. One was for walking rough ground, the other for crossing a hedge, river or whatever. So it was better than the thumb sticks other boys had. It was a beautiful burnished dark brown with a dark rusty hue. It looked really good, and so that boy decided he wanted it and made life awful for me. Why, I don't know. I was so careful I even had it in the sleeping bag with me so nobody could steal it. But nonetheless, he tried. That time I shouted and he ran off.'

Jason pauses for a deep breath. 'The following day, he just grabbed it while I was tying up a shoe lace. I went after him and tussled with him to get it back, but he tripped me up into a muddy shallow pool. I was soaked and dirty but still I went straight after him. By then, he was with three other boys, all tall and strong. I rushed up and grabbed my stick. We tussled again and he kicked and punched me. Where my strength came from, I don't know. But I managed to pull the stick away. And he came after me again so I whacked him with it really hard. Enraged, I did it again, and again, stopping him in his tracks. On the last blow across his back, he turned and ran back to his friends. I was so angry I threw the stick into the river, I don't know why, but I just watched it wash downstream.'

'Wow, you taught him a lesson! Good on you, well done!' Abby pats his side and smiles.

'But, it didn't finish there, though. He reported me, showed the marks on his back to the teacher, and I had to face the beak. I insisted *he* was in the wrong and always bullied *me*, but nobody listened, and I was caned. They didn't even question him. Caned in front of the whole school during assembly— as a lesson to others; imagine that! Everyone was laughing at me. That's why I hate the place!'

'How awful. It's a most unjust world, Jason. But you must do your best to forget or ignore them. Let's think of going crabbing on Thursday. Got to be positive, mate,' she touches him on the arm. 'Let's have some more crab, it's delicious, and the cake looks great,' she continues brightly but with an expression of concern.

Jason cuts a big slice of Aunty's home-made fruit cake each and they eat it with gusto, licking their fingers clean. Once they have had their fill, she goes to thank Uncle and Aunty and he shows her to the door. Then he walks to the main road and halfway down the hill with her, then she stops. 'See you for the tide on Thursday,' she says, 'and thanks so much for inviting me. Hope it's made you feel positive!' She gives him a little peck on the cheek, turns and goes her own way home.

In her bed that night, Abby lies awake looking at the ceiling, considering Jason's predicament at school. It's such a contrast when she pictures him at his happiest, amongst nature at low tide. She thinks of the enjoyable times they spend hunting under the water probing in hidden ledges and holes where the unknown lurks, and falls asleep contentedly.

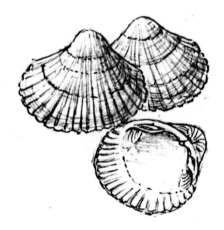

Cockles

Chapter Eight

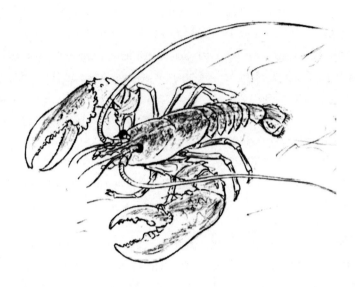

Bull (Cock) Lobster

Experience and Frustration

That evening, Jason sits quietly in his room. His treasured guide is open, but he is all too aware of the pile of homework he has to finish before returning to school in eight days' time. His good intentions to complete it all in the first few days of the holiday have gone astray. All the previous week, he was distracted visiting the library and museum, or writing and sketching the sea shore. He has sent a postcard and another letter to his parents, but schoolwork has been pushed to one side. Again, he looks at his unopened satchel. It is almost the last thing he sees before going to sleep.

His anxiety gets him up early the next morning and he sets up the small desk in his room ready to commence work. He plans to spend the next three days diligently applying himself to the unwanted task so all can be complete before the low tides start on Thursday. Before eight, he is looking at his books to plan the time for each of the subjects he has to address, and decides to start on his least favourite, algebra.

He makes a good start, but when the sun breaks through the clouds and fills his room with joyous morning light, his mind begins to drift. Half way through the second equation, he stops, downs his pen and slips downstairs. Silently, he unlatches the front door and sneaks out and up the road to where Old Joe should be taking the morning sun.

'Morning, Mr Joe,' he calls cheerily as he approaches the old man, then stands motionless awaiting a response. Did he speak clearly or loudly enough? He watches the old man whose arm and hand movements seem even slower than ever. Joe seems confused for a few moments, but then he appears to gaze towards Jason.

'Are you the young thing singing in church recent Sunday mornings? Your voice is so bold and clear. Aah! to be young,' Joe says in feeble tones.

'I caught a lobster last Saturday. Nearly two pounds! It was in the hole in the gully; the one you told me about. The day before, I had a nice crab there!' Jason tells him excitedly. 'And I caught loads of prawns around the wreck. But most amazing of all, in the big hole was a conger, a huge thing, and a lobster, a bright deep blue, so beautiful. They seem to be living together.' His effusion leaves him breathless. Though he knows he told Joe of this outside the church on Easter Sunday, he doubts if the old man would remember.

Joe chuckles quietly to himself as he drifts back to his own days on the rocks. He recalls these days well, yet he is less sure about any recent events or conversations. Then again, he utters in a quiet wheezy voice, 'Conger and lobster, often together, particularly there; he waits for the lobster to shed, and while it's soft he eats it, cunning old devil. A bully of the undersea world, ya know. Often someone gaffs him out first, maybe that lot from East End Farm.'

'I think this lobster is too big for even Jack to eat—that's what I named the conger,' Jason says. 'I could see the lobster clearly, a huge body, a cow definitely. Do you think she might have eggs?'

'Ah, yah, certainly, we always caught berried hens in the spring. Call them berries cos the eggs look like tiny berries, thousands of them. Never take those. Always leave them for eggs to hatch, that's the future stock of lobsters,' Joe says with more vigour as his memories perk him up.

'Oh, I didn't even attempt to catch her once I saw her,' Jason assures him. 'She is the most beautiful blue imaginable. I hope she's safe now. There are no big spring tides until the end of summer. And I hope I can come back here then.'

Joe looks a little more animated. 'Aye, aye, August springs will be the next. If the weather is fine, ye can walk to the wreck, and then it's full of lobsters, prawns and congers. But people fight to get there first for the good pickings. The rough devils from East End Farm, maybe the ones ye saw, have always fought with their cousins from Wespalone, the other side of the headland—it's a family feud. That's why I've always had a run in with the East End lot, cos I'm related to the others—the men who help me to church. Yes, keep ye distance from East mob,' he advises as his eyes open wider in a more alert gaze.

Jason nods and thinks for a moment about this, then he says, 'The tides this week are not so low, but is it still worth looking at low tide?'

'Aye, certainly, plenty of good places on these tides if ye know where to go. Listen, boy. If tide ebbs the big rock off Traxi Point, that's the west point of ye bay, then start looking between there and Blackledge. Doubt if you've looked there before. Ye'll find fifty yards around the point is a gully with three pools. Look in the middle one facing east. Then there's a crack parallel to land, fifty yards from the cliff; about six feet deep. About twenty good crab holes there on either side. Then three narrow gullies run from sea to cliff. One or two good holes; always look for twists in the strata...' Joe rambles on, with amazing detail and recall.

Jason has brought his notebook with Joe's previous revelations and is soon writing rapidly, making quick sketches as more the old man's intimate knowledge unfolds. Joe continues describing each rock and gully where crabs, lobsters and prawns can be found. Jason says nothing to interrupt Joe's monologue, but listens intently, scribbling everything possible down. 'And ye won't see those bullies, they never bother on smaller tides. They'll be working on farms, a busy time of year,' Joe continues, shaking his head.

'Why are they bullies?' Jason says tentatively.

'Bullies, everywhere in people and nature. Take advantage of anyone, anything. Call it natural selection; survival of fittest. Eh, when I was young bullies picked on me. Then I went to sea, became tough, could see anyone off; and I did, often. Now I'm old and infirm the devils hound me again, those boys is 'orrid, 'orrid ! Look at that conger, a bully; magpies bully smaller birds. They saw off a beautiful turtle dove this week; hounded her off the nest. Ate her eggs, bullies! If magpies were good to eat everyone would shoot them; but to eat they taste as sour as their character. It's what they call nature,' Joe drifts on, gazing into oblivion as his mind scans the decades of times past.

'I've been bullied, so I try to keep myself to myself. It's why I love the solitude out on the rocks away from everyone, or most people. But next week, I'll be back in school. I hate the thought of it...' Jason says, his voice quavering a little. Then he feels more positive. 'Thank you, Mr Joe. I'll bring you a nice dressed crab if I catch any. I've lots of homework to do in the next few days, but I'll make sure it's all done before the tides. Thank you, Mr Joe.' And he walks away with a new spring in his step, clutching his notebook.

Jason arrives back to find Gertie and Charles sitting at the breakfast table. 'We were about to send a search party for you. I came to your room to find it empty!' Gertie says surprised.

'Oh, I'm sorry, I just went to see Joe quickly, and he started to tell me about another area on the rocks to try this week. His descriptions are amazing, still such a sharp memory at his age. So, I just had to listen and take notes.'

'Never mind,' says Gertie. 'Breakfast is all ready, I'll just fry the eggs now.'

The three eat then Jason excuses himself to carry on with his homework. In his room, his face screws up as he looks at the list of algebra he hopes to complete by lunchtime. So he concentrates and quickly gets himself into studious mode and smiles as he writes QED for the second time.

'Quod erat demonstrandum!' he whispers and smiles to himself. 'Only three more to go.' But then his notebook takes his attention for a second and he cannot resist looking at the scribbles he jotted in haste.

He starts to fill out one of the sketches he made, using his imagination to give intricate detail including one of a large flat boulder at an angle to the base of a narrow cleft, and the sandy corner that Joe said was a favourite lair for large crabs and occasionally a lobster.

The power of his imagination begins to flow and he doodles on other notes, then starts to draw a crab, lobster and a fiddler. Suddenly, he realises over an hour has passed, and how he is falling further behind with his work schedule. He puts the notebook under his pillow and looks at the next equation he has to work out. But within half an hour, his head is flat on the desk and he is fast asleep.

He is woken when Aunty calls him for lunch, which refreshes him for a short while. He carries on working, looking at the history questions in between sessions of algebra, but cannot get back into the stride of the morning. His progress is tediously slow, even though he continues trying until called for supper.

It is well into the third day when he completes the algebra, having slogged all morning at history, and now he has to look at his English homework. After a quick lunch of ham and cheese sandwiches, he opens the envelope with the questions set by his master who is nicknamed Fagin, after the part he played in his school play long ago. He is the one master who seems to engage all the class, just as Fagin did to tempt his boys into criminal pranks. He starts writing quickly his account of the anonymous Scottish poem 'Sir Patrick Spens'.

He loves this for the excitement it conveys and knowledge it shows of the mood changes of the weather, just like the vivid account of the Stenvetia, and for the drama of the sad and heroic ending. Having gained his first experience of the sea's power, he can imagine how so many tales on the high seas could end this way. In just the short time staying on the coast, he has seen the changing moods of the tides, and the effect on the creatures that inhabit the shores. Quietly, he reads it aloud to himself seeing it vividly.

The first word that Sir Patrick read
Sae loud, loud laucht he;
The neist word that Sir Patrick read
The tear blindit his ee.

'O wha is this has duin this deed
An tauld the king o me,
Tae send us out, at this time o year,
Tae sail abuin the sea?

'Be it wind, be it weet, be it hail, be it sleet,
Our ship maun sail the faem;
The King's dauchter o Noroway,
Tis we maun fetch her hame.'

They hoystit their sails on Monenday morn,
Wi aw the speed they may;
They hae landit in Noroway
Upon a Wodensday.

'Mak ready, mak ready, my merry men aw!
Our gude ship sails the morn.'
'Nou eer alack, ma maister dear,
I fear a deadly storm.'

'A saw the new muin late yestreen
Wi the auld muin in her airm
And gif we gang tae sea, maister,
A fear we'll cam tae hairm.'

They hadnae sailt a league, a league,
A league but barely three,
When the lift grew dark, an the wind blew loud
An gurly grew the sea.

The ankers brak, an the topmaist lap,
It was sic a deadly storm.
An the waves cam ower the broken ship
Til aw her sides were torn.

And lang, lang may the maidens sit
Wi their gowd kames in their hair,
A-waitin for their ane dear loes!
For them they'll see nae mair.

Half-ower, half-ower to Aberdour,
Tis fifty fathoms deep;
An there lies gude Sir Patrick Spens,
Wi the Scots lords at his feet!

He writes two pages about the poem with vivid imagination and is pleased when he finishes with The End. He then turns the question paper over to see the list of essays includes the title "My Holidays". Quickly, he lists six headings and within ten minutes, he is writing profusely.

He has tea with Charles and Gertie just after four and they can see he is anxious, with so many thoughts, dreams and expectations in his mind.

'Done all those equations yet?' Charles asks.

'At last! Algebra is hard work, but I've finished history as well and am now writing my English essay,' Jason says positively.

They are both amazed when he scampers back upstairs to continue his homework. In between writing every few paragraphs, he picks up the notebook and starts another sketch of a pool, a rock formation, the wreck and all the other features he can recall, including every single crab and lobster hole. He gives names to some of the places where he has caught something: the high ledge, coffin rock, the deep shelf, and the secret hole, where Jack and Matilda reside. He knows it will be a long while before he sees Jack and Matilda again, indeed if ever.

He decides to have a walk to the sea wall to look at the full tide at five thirty, not put off by the thought of another possible encounter with Skipper Jonny. He looks at some dark clouds in the sky and hopes it's not an omen of bumping into Skipper Jonny or that it will be raining the next day. He doesn't want anything to ruin the first day of crabbing tides for over a week. But then a few spots of rain begin to fall and he runs back home, hoping this will not continue for his last few days of holiday.

On arrival, he is greeted by an aroma from the oven.

Immediately, he wonders what treat will be served tonight. After a quick wash, he is back at the table where Charles is reading the evening newspaper. Several minutes later he puts it down and shakes his head.

'Let's hope the new Prime Minister has more successes than the last! Eh, Jason?' he looks at the lad whose mind is obviously elsewhere. 'Ye just can't wait to go fishing again, I bet.'

Gertie enters wearing an apron. 'Fishing will be when all homework is complete! I've promised Mum and Dad that I shall ensure it is all done. So, how's it coming on, Jason?'

'I'll be finished before breakfast! I've just a few more paragraphs to write and then it's all complete, and my satchel can be packed!' he says rather smugly.

'That's good, well done. So now we can all now enjoy the mutton chops for supper,' Gertie says, somewhat relieved, 'and I suppose you will require a packed fishing lunch tomorrow?'

'Yes, please! I just hope it's not raining,' Jason sighs, but is full of anticipation.

The meal is generous and filling. All agree the mutton is delicious, particularly with herb gravy, roasted potatoes, mashed swede and sprouts. Aunty's special steamed lemon pudding concludes yet another memorable meal for Jason. After helping to clear the table and the washing up, Jason heads off to bed.

All night, he dreams of his adventures on the low tide and discovering new places as vast areas of rocks, pools and weed filled gullies are uncovered. He imagines setting off in a small boat and drifting for hours on a silky sea with little sign of life in any direction but for the slow methodical flashing of a solitary lighthouse on a distant island.

He drifts for hours watching a single gannet cruising on the thermals in its search for a shoal of fish. In the distance, a lone dolphin surfaces in its characteristic series of rolls, with the sickle dorsal fin cutting a sharp ripple through the gentle swells. An adroit cuttlefish with tentacles fully extended swims by in search of prey; it slowly sinks into the blue-green depths. A sleek gunmetal coloured tope swims effortlessly by in its hunt for shoals of seasonal fish, and carries on towards the distant horizon.

Finally, he cruises into a sheltered bay on the deserted island where the electrically charged lighthouse still sends its flashing messages to nobody. The shallow water in the bay is multi-coloured with myriad varieties of sea life hiding under numerous different hues of green, brown and red seaweeds. He beaches the boat on a shingle beach and wades through the water that is filled with darting translucent prawns, twitching shrimps, symmetrical blue-black mussels, spiral winkles and whelks, and flat round oysters, all thriving on the pure water that's laden with fine dusty clouds of algae and plankton that will feed them all season.

As he wades through the water, he sees the marine life extending before him and he feels so close to it. He knows this solitary searching is the life he wishes to lead, away from the crowds of people who will push and bully him in pursuit of their greedy goals. Then he opens his eyes and gazes at the ceiling as the first rays of sunlight stream through a gap in the curtains.

He leaps out of bed and looks out across the bay, where the swirling sea is just beginning to ebb. Perhaps this will be the first day when he can again search the rocks for its treasures. It's the Thursday after Easter Sunday, and soon his long holiday will come to an end, so he hopes these last few days will be successful.

He sits with Charles and Gertie and devours two poached eggs on toast for breakfast. Following his Uncle's example, he sprinkles Worcestershire Sauce onto the yolks.

'I thought you'd like something more today to fuel your energy for crabbing,' Gertie says. 'I'm so pleased you have completed the homework, well done, Jason!'

'Aye, good lad,' Charles says, patting Jason's back. 'Now you can really enjoy fishing the last few tides. It'll be so good if you can take a few crabs home. I bet my brother hasn't tasted one for donkey's years!'

'Now you get off so there's plenty of time before low tide, good luck!' Aunty says, willing him onwards.

'Thanks for a lovely breakfast, Aunty,' Jason says, 'and I do like the sauce on the egg. I hope I'll bring back something for supper! I'll see you later.' And off he scurries.

Late morning, he is sitting on the limestone shelves near Traxi Point waiting to see if the crabbing rocks will be uncovered. Joe has told him the features on the headland that indicate the extent of the ebb. In the middle of the bay, he knows the location of the three pools where he caught a haversack of prawns. They should soon be exposed and he waits eagerly for a sign of the reefs and rocks that define the new places that old Joe so vividly described to him.

The tide is ebbing at a far slower pace than the previous spring tides before so he knows that perhaps only a few holes will reveal this day. On the next two days, the tides will uncover more areas for him to search. But that will be it—on Sunday, he will be heading back to the Midlands to start school, so he has limited time to relish the life he has grown to enjoy so much.

As he is mesmerised by the swirling currents around each outcrop of weedy rocks, he realises that the hours of ebb tide are ticking away, and hopes of foraging might remain out of reach, as all the creatures will be safely covered by the water. There is now a far smaller stretch of the shelving rocks than was uncovered on the previous spring tides, and it all looks very different with just few patches of weed-strewn rocks to search. He walks towards the west corner of the bay but the rock Joe said to look for remains covered. He wades into the tide above his knees where the serrated wrack washes gently to and fro in a vast carpet, below which numerous creatures could be hiding; many must be so close yet are completely hidden.

He thinks out loud, 'So near, yet so far. I know they are there, but just out of reach, like so much in life!'

He wades deeper, trying to spot anything wedged in the rocks. He realises the swirling sea and diffused sunlight playing on the fronds of seaweed is confusing his vision, and the chance of finding something is becoming more remote.

He stands waist deep with the water swashing around his body and his dreams of solitude flash back. But then, looking back to the shore in the distance, he sees the first of the coaches that arrive daily around noon, cruising down the hill into the field.

The day trippers tumble into the car park, and like a line of ants, they file down onto the sands and accumulate in groups to take in the fresh sea air and play games on the sands. They have their lunches packed in wicker baskets and old army grips, all set to satisfy themselves for the day. But none of them knows the secrets that Jason has discovered from his searching and Old Joe's guidance over the rocks. Nor do they comprehend the great mysteries and challenges that the hidden areas can pose, where he stands alone in hope.

He wades across to the middle of the bay where the prawn pools would be, but the three are merged into one by the sluggish tide that will not fall away. He prods around with his net and spots many small shapes zipping away and disappearing out into the deep water. He tries scooping under many of the large flat stones, but as they are covered by nearly two feet of water, all his attempts are in vain. He scowls knowing that the ebb cannot be speeded up, but soon notices the first surges of gentle waves as the sea begins to flood once again. He frowns at the hopelessness of his situation. Slowly, he returns to the shore in his sodden shorts, his haversack empty for the first time. He sits and quickly eats his sandwiches, then sets off homewards.

He passes the gathering groups on the beach as they arrange their deck chairs and unpack their picnic lunches and thermos flasks of tea and coffee and chatter incessantly among themselves. He is determined not hear the quips and questions blurted at him.

'What ya caught, boy? Bag looks empty,' one calls.

He ignores this and the subsequent laughter and carries on the path to Parson's Wood that will take him up the long flight of steps through the woods to the road at the summit of the hill. He does not have the usual bounce in his stride as he trudges up every step. Towards the top, he turns and looks back over the bay where the tide is flooding sluggishly, and ponders silently. He knows tomorrow the tide will be far lower and there'll be plenty of ledges, pools and crevices to search, so perhaps he will have a good catch. With that in mind he aims to finish the few paragraphs of remaining homework so he will have a full day of rock fishing the next day.

When he arrives home shortly after one thirty, his shorts have dried. Instead of changing and taking a bath, he sits at his desk and begins writing. His imagination takes him into unknown areas of the sea and the words flow continually for a few hours. Later in the afternoon, Gertie hears sounds from the bathroom and hopes it is a signal that Jason might have finished his work. At about four thirty, he comes down stairs looking refreshed, and it is time for tea. Gertie calls Charles in from the garden, and the three sit together.

On the table, there is a whole, warm bara brith, and a plate of thin-looking golden scones studded sparsely with currants. Jason sits and takes in the wafts of freshly-baked food.

'What are these?' he asks Aunty. 'Something new again?'

Gertie smiles as Charles walks in and pick up one of the scones. 'Cor, lovely! And still warm from the griddle!' he beams, picking up a second.

Jason looks at him enquiringly.

'Welsh cakes! Not had one of these before?' Jason shakes his head.

'Hey, Gertie, this lad's not tasted Welsh cakes, can you believe it? Maybe he's never tried faggots either!' Charles says, and he gives away the surprise of the evening's supper.

Jason eats a Welsh cake quickly and takes a second. 'Delicious eh, Jason? Gertie has her own recipe for these. Tell him, Gertie, and perhaps he can make them at home.'

'Oh, it's a standard recipe, but I put in extra butter and spices, that's all. I'll write it down for you,' Gertie says.

'This feast has given me the strength to carry on with my homework,' says Jason. 'I think I can finish it now.'

That's excellent, darling,' says Gertie, 'I'm proud of your determination.'

At six thirty, having finished the last essay and packed his satchel into his case, Jason comes down for supper. Indeed it is faggots and peas with onion gravy and mashed potatoes. Charles tucks in with relish, then helps himself to a second faggot. Jason is a little more hesitant at first but once he has a few forkfuls combining the three, he eats with more enthusiasm.

'These are not nearly as strong as ones we have at home, which have a very livery taste,' Jason remarks. 'These are lighter and much nicer. They're just mildly livery and have sweetness from something, they're actually delicious!'

'Llewellyn the butcher is very proud of his faggots!' Gertie laughs. 'He won't give the recipe to anyone—but they are very popular.'

'You bet, they are really tasty, and the peas don't make my mouth feel fizzy, either. Why is that, Aunty?' Jason enquires.

'Well, some people put far too much bi-carb in when soaking them.'

'Bi-carb?'

'Bi-carbonate of soda,' Charles cuts in. 'Lots of people use it when cooking cabbage because it keeps the green colour. But Gertie only uses a little salt, and that's why all her cooking is so tasty, agree?'

'Yes, certainly!' Jason says, while Gertie looks a tad embarrassed by all this praise.

For a few moments, they are all silent, content after such a fine meal.

Then Jason stretches. 'Well, I must go to bed now, I feel a bit too full for pudding, if that is all right? It was all those lovely Welsh cakes and bara brith for tea. But thanks for another delicious meal! Good night, Uncle, Aunty,' and with that he heads upstairs to bed.

The air is clear and the sky blue and bright the next morning as Jason walks onto the beach, full of expectation as the sea is ebbing more briskly. There's a group of youngsters sitting on a clump of rocks to the left basking in the morning sun and one waves eagerly to Jason. It is Abby, who did not appear the previous day. She and her friends jabber away and laugh loudly as they plan their daily exploits. She waves again, then after five minutes. she splits from the raucous gathering and skips over towards Jason.

'G'day, should be a decent low tide later. Going to the usual place, cos I'll come and see you?' she says, smiling broadly.

'Hello! I was here yesterday, but it wasn't any use as the tide didn't go out very far. Today, it's a lot better. I'll be going from that corner rock, yonder, known locally as Traxi Point,' he indicates with an outstretched arm, 'and then heading towards Blackledge, ending up there. Plenty of holes to look for; I've got it all correctly planned, so let's hope!'

'Sure, there was low pressure yesterday after the dull few days, but today, it's up by nearly ten bars. Always check the glass every morning— it's so very different today and for the next few,' she says with authority.

Jason looks rather nonplussed.

'Come on, high pressure pushes the tide down and it goes out further. Logical eh? Always look for high pressure when going yabbie digging. Give them a foot of water and little devils are in their element, you'll never catch them. Same here, I guess.'

'Well, it was hopeless yesterday. Two foot of water over the pools. I didn't have a chance! Just got soaked again and finished up with an empty sack!' Jason says with a grin. 'But let's see what today brings. I'll be at Blackledge in about an hour or so. I'll be starting at Traxi,' he points at the headland.

'Yup, I'll come and see you there. Good luck!' And then Abby trots back to her noisy friends.

Jason clambers around the corner in accordance with Joe's instructions, and when he sees the gully with three pools, and knows he is on the right spot. He puts on his swimming costume and packs his clothes in a small shoulder bag. He feels the sun's warmth on his back and thighs as he scurries over the barnacled rocks towards the tide. In the first few holes, everything he sees is quite small and nowhere near the legal size. In the deep cleft, he does find a pair of crabs which he assesses are on the borderline of the legal size so leaves them in their hiding place. Then in a series of ledges where the rock comes to the side of the gully, he finds two handsome crabs, so has something in his haversack before he has travelled too far. By the time he is approaching Blackledge, he has caught a further crab; the bag is bulging once more and he feels proud again.

He realises that his attention has focused on the crab places Joe described and that he has not searched for the less obvious lobster holes and ledges. These he knows are more difficult to spot as the secretive crustacean lives under the water, well shrouded by dangling wrack, oar weed and long sea belt. He is not carrying his notebook for fear of dropping it into a pool, or getting it soaked, and then all the precious notes might be lost, but before setting out, he committed all the essentials to memory. He thinks carefully of the description Joe gave him of a long narrow pool with a high rock either side, which he said would be close to the east side of Blackledge.

As low tide is approaching, he sees many herring gulls stomping across the rocks and lots of black and white oyster catchers scampering in and out of the clefts, their orange bills working overtime as they turn small pebbles and shells in search of sand hoppers and small crabs. Every now and again, a gull heaves a soft crab from a cleft, immediately to be surrounded by many of its fellows, all eager to partake in the feast.

Voraciously, each crab is torn to shreds and devoured. They also peck at the soft centres of starfish, leaving the horny arms abandoned. But so many birds on the rocks tells Jason that the area has not been disturbed by anybody, so he should have the first picking at all the holes.

The wreck seems far in the distance with a great swathe of tide between it and the land, so many of the holes remain covered on this small spring tide. He gazes to where the secret hole would be covered by several feet of water and wonders.

The rocks are traversed by a series of deep clefts from the contorted strata of the limestone and each of these has fissures, cracks and depressions where crabs can hide. Methodically, he works his way along every narrow gully, finding numerous crabs. As before, many are undersized, but his eyes quickly attune to recognise the sizeable ones, and he wastes no time easing out any that are too small. His haversack soon contains another three crabs of decent size.

One of the narrow gullies he has not explored before has a shallow sandy pool and there is something different about its appearance. The water to one end is inky dark with a mist of black hovering where a clump of bladder wrack hangs in long twisted fronds. He recalls Joe instructing him to look in this place and particularly for the sooty water in the corner of the pool, for this could be caused by a lobster, buried in the deep black silt that settles in clefts and corners. He recalls Joe's tale of this pool, saying that it's rare to catch more than one lobster each year in this place. Gingerly, he eases the seaweed away to see a pair of red antennae twitching in the dark corner beneath.

It's a narrow crack and he tries to ease his hook to the side to probe well behind where he believes the creature will be settled. As he does, the flash of the elliptical orange edges of the pair of claws glints from the blackness. It seems to be a fine lobster with a shell as dark as the inky lair. Through the murkiness, he sees the proboscis, the dark eyes and cylindrical carapace easing outwards in curiosity. Then it spots the danger of the sunlight and Jason's shadow, and it suddenly shoots backwards with a flick of its tail, sending a cloud of black silt into the pool. It has retreated to the safety of its hole and is nowhere to be seen.

Jason tries to locate it by probing the tip of the hook at every angle into the depths, but to no avail— it seems to have eluded him. Frustrated after ten wasted minutes, he sighs heavily and decides to continue his searches in the many other pools and ledges waiting to be explored.

He keeps looking back to the lobster pool but his wandering takes him around the tide mark to another area Joe had described. He locates a long gully formed from the tilted strata where there are several crevices for larger crabs to hide in, and he searches these methodically. But this takes him out of sight of the rocks where he missed the lobster.

When he looks at the summit of the cliff, he spots the familiar shape of Abby waving to him as he turns to head back to have another attempt at catching the elusive lobster. But as he rounds the corner to the rocks of Blackledge, to his horror he spots a wiry short-haired lady with army-issue shorts bending close to where he saw the lobster. She is talking to someone. Then he sees a short, stocky man with a bald head and similar shorts clambering from the gully. Jason can tell there is something in his net, which he then deposits into the sack the lady is holding open for him. Jason can see they have a lobster—it has to be the one he missed. He stamps his foot on the rocks in frustration.

'That was *my* lobster!' he shouts, even though nobody but he can hear him. As the pair head towards him, the man splashes into a large pool, where he bends down and quickly pulls out a nice pair of crabs. These too are wrapped in weed, and deposited into to the sack. Then they see Jason heading towards them carrying a bag containing his own catch.

'Had a good catch, laddie? Trust they are all big enough, the legal size that is,' the man calls to him. 'I'll need to inspect them, please,' he adds officiously, quickly displaying an official Sea Fisheries permit.'

'Of course, they are!' Jason replies indignantly as the pair approaches him, and he opens his haversack to show a large bull crab on the top.

The man pulls it out and also inspects the two others he can easily see. 'Hmmm, yes, all right—they are a good size. They must all be over four and a half inches—you *do* know that, don't you?' he says with no humour or friendliness.

'Yes, of course I know that, and what's more, I saw that lobster in the hole earlier and was on my way back to catch it!' Jason says, quivering with anger and frustration. 'I was just waiting for the murky water to clear.'

'Oh, it takes a *real* expert to get them out!' the lady interrupts. 'Particularly there; few can catch them from that place, and many other holes are the same. When you have been coming here for as long as we have, perhaps you could be an expert too!' she continues patronisingly.

Jason is quick with his riposte. 'I caught a lobster on the last tides. It was over two pounds!' So there, he adds under his breath. He is furious they have caught the very one he failed to winkle out earlier, but tries not to show it. Then he sees Abby approaching, and bids them farewell. 'Must go now, good afternoon, so nice to meet you!' he says determinedly, but his spirits begin to crumble as he walks over to greet Abby.

'That man caught my lobster!' he says in anger. 'I saw it first and was coming back to catch it, but they sneaked in. That was *my* lobster.'

Seeing his irritation, Abby tries to calm him. 'But you've a full bag, a nice few crabs— that's amazing in itself. Can't get everything, the rocks are free after all, so he was the lucky one today. Be your turn next time, don't worry!'

'She said he was an expert, well I'll show them, I'll be an expert, better than them, you wait!' he says as his blushing face shows the frustration he feels. 'They were so smug and condescending too. And they behaved as though I couldn't be expected to know the regulations about size. But I do. Both Joe and Uncle have told me.'

'It looked to me as though you were credible to them,' Abby says.

'Well, yes, I suppose I was.'

'So you didn't let them bully you, did you?'

Jason is silent for a moment or two. 'No, no, I didn't!' But the man did, a bit, Jason says to himself.

Abby gives him an encouraging smile. 'Look at the wreck,' she says changing the subject, 'barely two foot sticking out, so anything there is sure safe. Bet that couple don't know your secret hole either...'

Jason looks out to sea and stands by Abby as the sea begins to swirl rapidly past the wreck, signalling the flooding tide. He takes a few breaths to calm down.

'Joe said it won't be till late August that we'll be able to get out there again,' he says in a more measured voice, 'so let's hope Jack and Matilda are safe and cosy in their undersea garden until then; nobody else can get there,' he smiles at Abby, and they both fix their eyes on the wreck, as slowly it disappears beneath the surging sea. 'Come on, I'll walk home with you. Maybe Aunty will bring us tea and some lovely cake!'

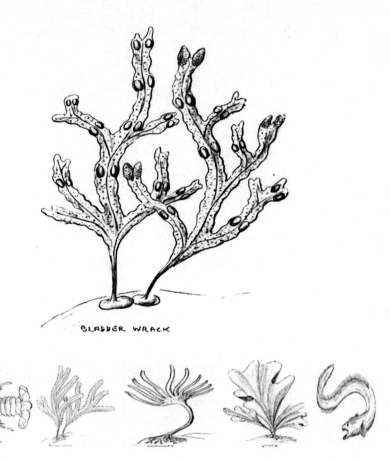

BLADDER WRACK

Chapter Nine

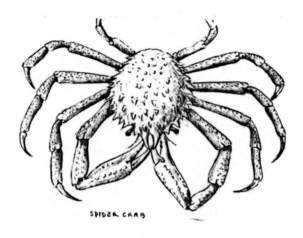

Spider Crab

Survival of the Strongest

Below the sea, time passes with the eternal ebb and flow of the tides, and the changing seasonal hours of light and darkness.

The lazy longer days of summer bring many new species to the tidal rocks. On their seasonal migrations, many are seeking places to settle and breed, or to cast their shells. This leaves the rocks and shores strewn with the debris of many sea creatures and the excess growth of marine vegetation. Slow-moving tides do not scour the rocks as do the high springs and seasonal gales. There is a waft of sun-drenched seaweed drifting over coastal areas. Old Joe sniffs the air every morning and knows that a decent blow is needed to clear the shores.

Under the sea, safe from the human scavengers of the low tide, Jack the conger eel and Matilda the large cow lobster reside in peace; but around them is an invasion that litters the sea bed with numerous cast shells. The fiddlers and shore crabs have been moulting for many weeks, but there is no vigorous tidal flow to wash empty shells away. The spider crabs all fight for a place to hang onto the rocks while they gorge on the plentiful growth of weed. They hang in great clusters, and although their puny claws can do no damage to each other or any of the other creatures competing for space, their sheer weight of numbers brings them superiority and most other creatures move away.

They moult in huge numbers but the soft ones are protected by a wall of hundreds of spiny ten-limbed creatures tangled together. It takes an opportunist large bass to bludgeon into them suddenly and swiftly grab a succulent jelly-shelled prize, then dart away at lightning speed. Other predators such as tope and huss have already taken their fill of shore crabs and now search for other prey.

Jack the conger peers out of his dark cave at a tangle of legs and spindly bodies piled across the bed before him. He has been morose for several weeks as his jaw slowly healed, with a thick layer of cartilage building up over the severed bone. Stealthily, he heads out with a mere quiver of his tail fins that propels him slowly forward. He slithers over the mounds of empty shells and across weed-covered rocks, ignoring the multitude of spiders clinging to the stumps of the horsetail. After endless searching, he spots a lone individual retreating among the discarded carapaces. He can detect by its bright colour that it has recently shed and is seeking some cover plus loose seaweed to decorate and camouflage its body. In one scoop, the large lump of jelly-soft crab disappears into his extended gullet. He cruises silently on.

Back in the hole they share, Matilda starts to creep towards the entrance. Her tail is fully extended, fanning water over the large brood of many thousands of eggs that are close to hatching. Though they appear to be hanging lifelessly under the umbrella of her tail, as the embryos grow they turn from black towards an orange tinge. She has a mother's intuitive sense and knows that soon the juveniles will start to emerge from their tiny eggs.

For well over twenty years she has, each season, produced such a crop, and it has increased successively every time as her body mass has increased. She fans her swimmerets constantly, so every egg will get enough fresh water and oxygen to develop and finally to induce hatching.

Jack has been absent a long while and Matilda creeps right to the entrance of the hole where she can feel the gentle flow of the tide. With her back arched high and claws splayed to elevate her body further, she detects the bursting of the first egg shell and a tiny pin-head size creature flexes its minuscule body for the first time. It is so light that it drifts upwards on the gentle current assisted by her continual fanning of the water. A second and third are quickly followed by a number of small clusters of the planktonic creatures.

Returning from his nightly hunt, Jack snaps the water with his great jaws but the showers of Matilda's progeny elude him and drift away into the darkness. With a thrust of his tail, he barges past Matilda, nudging her sideways. She flaps her tail to regain composure and this sends a cloudburst of young lobsters off on their tortuous voyage. She lifts herself sideways onto the stippled wall of the cave where she can anchor herself firmly and continue activating the hatching eggs. Agitated, Jack swooshes his mighty tail, causing a whirl that only sends the young more speedily into the open sea.

The baby lobsters continue to hatch for many hours. As the sky lightens with dawn, the sun sends its refreshing beams of gold through the diffused algae-rich green sea. Numerous shoaling fish gather to scoop up all the plankton they can, which includes many of Matilda's offspring.

Matilda sits alert with her claws flexing, resolutely ignoring the mighty Jack and the many small rockfish that are hopeful of a quick feed. She knows that once they are on their way her hatchlings are at the mercy of the tides and the numerous predators that they will meet on their long journey.

The tiny lobsters, with barely any resemblance to an adult, are to spend many weeks drifting on the currents. They will partake in the bounty of smaller plankton and algae that drift along the same route. Every few days, they will moult their exoskeletons and grow by a small amount, each time becoming stronger. Yet they are totally vulnerable to anything: jellyfish, larger plankton, and fish of every size from whitebait, sprats and mackerel to the mightiest basking shark.

Eventually, they begin to form an elongated shell, under a quarter of an inch long, that becomes firm, streamlined and weighty. At this point, they sink through the plankton to the sea bed. If they are not gobbled up on their way by any mid-water pelagic fish, such as bass, pollack, whiting, mullet and bream, as they land they are surrounded by a host of other bottom-dwelling species all looking for food.

If they settle on sand an army of plaice, flounders, dabs, sole, brill and many others will quickly devour them and none will survive. The fortunate few that settle on a rocky area have gobies, blennies, bull heads, rockling, gurnard, small bass and voracious shore crabs to contend with. Yet every year there are a few that manage to find a tiny crevice in which to hide alone, from where they can eventually become hunters themselves.

As the tiny lobsters grow, each of the frequent moults makes them most vulnerable. But gradually, their front legs become elongated into slender symmetrical claws evolved over millennia for defence and aggression. Slowly, with each shell cast, when the crustacean is still under an inch long, these become asymmetric, performing specific uses.

The larger has nodules for crushing prey. Ingeniously, bigger prey is gripped by the sharp ends of the pinchers, whereas smaller creatures can be gripped between the tip of the moveable pincer and the second notch of the rigid part of the claw, making it powerful and adaptable. The slender slicer claw has a sharp serrated edge to both parts and acts as an efficient chopper of the food crushed in the partner claw.

Goby

When barely two inches long, the baby lobster resembles an adult. Matilda has no idea how many will ever reach this stage, yet every year she keeps sending clouds of the minuscule plankton on their long path through life. Lobsters live at great depths, also hidden in the blackness of deep holes and ledges. Hence, they are away from the rays of the sun, and at these depths the red pigments of the sunlight do not penetrate the seawater. Hence, they are dark blue in colour, unlike any of the creatures of shallower waters. As the lobster grows so it becomes a more formidable hunter, yet its principle enemy then is often other lobsters competing for food on the same territory.

Darkness is now falling onto the oceans. After many hours of fanning, Matilda's tail slowly becomes lighter and lighter and she begins to flex it to the full for the first time in many months. She is exhausted and creeps into the blackness of the depth of the hole and settles into the soft silt. She has fed well over her time of brooding, benefitting from Jack's messy eating habit of leaving many half-eaten crabs and fish. Her body is full to bursting like a plump Victorian lady constricted in a tight corset. Yet for the moment, her solid armour contains the ever-expanding inner body and her brand-new skin.

In the dingy bleakness of her lair, while the stars shine in the inky sky above, she feels at last her shell has to give, yet there is no sign of her partner to provide protection for her. She tucks her tail under the carapace and extends her claws slowly, tumbling motionless onto one side. She feels the centre of her back slowly split from her proboscis to her segmented tail. Just as a Victorian lady is unlaced from her corset, so Matilda's flesh begins to bulge from the crack in the shell.

She barely twitches for a long while as slowly the shiny new bright-blue skin bursts out, pumped with water contained in the rest of the constricted body. The carapace splits into two, and the jelly-soft new carcass begins to ooze out. One by one, each leg is painstakingly withdrawn and the first of the slender red feelers quivers into freedom.

The segmented tail begins to emerge as the new vibrantly-coloured muscle is pulled from the old and the new body begins to take shape. It now is constricted only by its mighty claws that have to pass through the tiniest connecting joint to the carapace. All her effort has to go into preserving her magnificent claws and the muscle fluid is slowly sucked out of her old claws until miraculously the flesh is withdrawn.

Suddenly, in one, two, three hearty flaps of the tail, the two are in turn pulled free intact. Every feeler on the head and each hair on the tail is in place. The eyes, stomach, gills, and all internal organs are regenerated, and the empty exoskeleton of her entire old body lies discarded in the mud.

She is jelly soft and her new skin has to toughen rapidly or she runs the risk of attack from many marine creatures, great and small. Her instinct tells her to hide her discarded armour, just as any bird will deposit the shells of hatched egg far from the juveniles for fear of predators. She begins to stamp her soft legs in the squelchy sludge, sending a delicate cloud of murky blackness that oozes from the hole. The old shell is gradually dug deeper and deeper to make it inconspicuous until only a few leg and feeler tips protrude. She now settles to wait patiently for several weeks for the new shell to toughen and give her the basic protection she so urgently needs.

Her jaws are the first part to become harder, which enables her to eat. She nibbles at the legs of her old shell, ingesting the calcium it contains that will speed up the firming of the new skin. Her formidable body bulk is now over three pounds. Although she is defenceless, her highly-sensitive antennae pick up every tiny movement of possible predators, from minuscule sand shrimps to fiddle fish, tope, bass or the mighty tail of Jack that flexes menacingly close to her.

Hugging the side of the cave a large sole with its sandpaper-like skin and small muscular jaws creeps closer and closer to her. Several smaller dabs surround the sole as though about to make a formidable attack. Many crabs and a large dogfish approach the opening of the hole, but they have to encounter Jack before they have any chance of reaching the confined Matilda. With one great snap of his jaw, he sends a bull huss reeling into the darkness of the night. No fiddler or spider crab dares to come near. But Jack's acute sense of natural aromas tells him a crustacean has just cast its shell close by, and this inflames his appetite.

In her vulnerable state, Matilda nibbles at more legs from her own shell. Her senses are alert to any danger. The tiny eyes of many fish and small crustaceans set upon her, but only the large conger with whom she has shared this hole for so long poses any threat. She now faces the dilemma of whether to sit it out with hungry Jack, or escape the hole and go in search of another place of refuge and a mate. Once out of the cave, it is uncertain how many other large and voracious creatures she might encounter. It's a dilemma she faces every time she casts her shell. So far, she has survived.

A powerful angler fish has recently set up residence several yards away, close to the wreck. Here it can trick small and larger fish that pass into believing they have an easy supper of his false bait. For many fish, his bait is tempting, and they are snapped into the huge gaping mouth in a split second. The jaws will extend to swallow prey of considerable size, and Matilda's succulent body might be very appealing.

Despite this, she knows it is time to leave the hole. Her senses warn that Jack, in an alert posture with fins erect, jaws open and rows of dagger-like raised teeth, is searching for unsuspecting prey, and it could be her. Perhaps he will not be hungry at the critical time, but she cannot take any chances. She can move very stealthily, clinging to the side or the roof of her lair.

Nonetheless, as she inches a tiny step at the time towards the entrance to escape into the black of the night, Jack detects the tiniest vibrations from her body. He flexes his mighty girth as her feelers guide her slowly forward. Matilda senses Jack's posture is not friendly. She halts and retreats very slowly into the murkiness. Jack stays guarding the entrance of the hole with his mouth open to pick up any passing scents of a possible meal.

Two hours later, still in the dark of night, Matilda creeps from the depths once again. She detects Jack's tail is completely motionless and his fins are flat along the length of his body. She slips stealthily past and approaches the entrance, desperately aiming not to disturb him. He remains still as she passes his great yellow eyes with the black pupils staring blankly into nothing.

At last, she is out and feels the current of the flooding tide that brings a refreshing burst of water that's welcome after so long in the dankness of the hole. Her body begins to float as she glides free into the open water, mingling amongst the stems of the kelp. Now, she must search for a new refuge as quickly as possible.

After a few minutes, Jack's fins suddenly stand up and he springs awake. One flick of his great body propels him silently from the hole.

He gently beats the water with his great tail acting like a powerful rudder. He weaves through the forest of weed hugging the rocks to find a feed. His great eyes detect all moving creatures in the pitch black of the night, and the most tempting will be Matilda's succulent body. He opens his huge mouth and flexes his jaws to the fullest extent. He speeds forward, gliding over the undulating rocks until he spots her blue body scurrying amongst the weed.

She senses danger but before she can flap her tail to escape, he propels at her from behind. His jaws are wide open and his needle teeth raised, and she disappears in one great swallow—it is like a hungry man guzzling a huge bowl of spaghetti in one. The claws and feelers are the last to vanish into the darkness.

With a mighty heave of Jack's gullet, she is squeezed down into his stomach where immediately the sweet taste of the open sea turns into the sourness of the digestive acids.

She takes in the foul liquid that's devoid of oxygen and rapidly begins to suffocate. Soon the poison flows through her body to her central nerve, cauterising any feeling, and she drifts slowly into oblivion forever. The caustic attack scalds her bright-blue new soft shell, bleaching its colour as it begins to dissolve, satisfying the appetite of the voracious conger. It's just as a powerful businessman will swallow up other enterprises to increase his market strength, irrespective of whether they are friends or not.

Jack creeps back across the rocks to his lair where he can lie and digest the remains of Matilda in peace. Their long companionship has come to an abrupt end and she is no more, gone the way of so many of her species before her.

Conger Eel hunting

Days and nights pass until under the moonless sky there is a heavy reverberation across the rocks. The clunking together of the claws of a huge lobster act as acute warning signals for many creatures. Green and yellow-belly shore crabs and red-eyed velvet swimming crabs scurry into their holes as quickly as dancing sand crabs on tropical shores.

Coming across the undulating rocks is a large bull lobster called Jake. He has spent many months underneath the great shelving rocks of Blackledge. Submerged here are many deep retreats formed in the strata of the rock, and successfully hidden he has fed himself on the abundance of soft crabs and small fish. There is nothing he will not tackle for a hearty meal.

This bull lobster has mighty claws with a crusher designed for the toughest prey. He weighs over seven pounds and his body and claws are well over two feet long; considerably longer than Matilda and over double her weight.

In the dark of night, he sets out across the sand where he can grasp unsuspecting flatfish with the great claws. The sharp points of the slicer claw can dig through the sand to grasp unsuspecting fish firmly; only a very large one can escape. The crusher then comes rapidly into action and squeezes life from the victim. He takes them back to his lair to devour them over many weeks as their flesh rots away. Like a tweedy countryman who enjoys maggot-riddled game, he is a disgusting eater and relishes its putrefaction.

Now, however, he is setting off on a different mission, in search of the cow that has been his mate for many seasons. He left her with the eggs he fertilised many months before, not intending to see her again until the next mating season, when she changes her shell, and he senses this has just happened. He has not cast his shell for years; it has become so thick by building up numerous layers of calcium that it is now impenetrable. Whether he will ever go through moulting again is unlikely as he has reached his natural extent, but he is probably set to keep going for many years to come.

The bull lobster rumbles his way over the ledges and gullies with remarkable agility, as in water the huge claws are weightless. He can raise them high for an attack or as a warning to others. Fully splayed, the claws open to over four inches so he can grasp considerably sized prey. The angler fish, who has just confused and swallowed two large Dover sole, sees the mighty crustacean approaching and moves into the safety of deeper water.

Suddenly, Jake snaps his crusher into the sand and a large turbot far longer than himself is grasped close to the tail. The powerful fish flaps vigorously, thrashing from its hiding place, carrying Jake as it swims away. With such strength and vigour, the turbot could match the lobster, so wisely he lets the fish swim free. Jake carries on heading towards the hole where he left his mate all those months before.

The mighty head of the conger is set resolutely at the entrance of the hole and although it is motionless, Jake senses it could be aggressive. He squats among the weed and waits until the eel sets off on its nightly patrol of the area. Then silently, he creeps on tiptoe into the cave where he expects to find Matilda. But apart from a swarm of large rock prawns and two dabs, the hole is empty and the black silt is undisturbed.

Confused, he searches every small fissure in vain hope, but there is no sign of Matilda. He settles onto the soft mud on the bottom of the hole and begins to probe with his front pincer legs, sending a fine black murk across the silt and out into the open sea beyond the hole. He pulls a piece of carapace shell from the depths, followed by an empty leg. His movements cloud the area, and the conger picks up a scent that has a familiar odour.

Jake digs more pieces of shell from the mud. It is obvious that Matilda cast her armour at this spot, and he suspects she then made a meal for the great eel. He sits on the remains alert, with his claws splayed. There is a swash of water like a whirlpool as Jack charges back into his home and slithers into the depths where Jake awaits.

The conger stops short and they glare at each other like two sumo wrestlers with Jack the conger taking on Jake the lobster. A stand-off continues, with both motionless for half an hour until the eel slinks backwards out of harm's way. He turns and settles his head to guard the entrance.

The lobster then detects the gentle fanning of a tail disturbing the water as it settles a little way in front of him. Stealthily, he edges forward contemplating a probable encounter. The large conger can detect all movement, but as it has a massive girth and the great spade of a tail, it defies attack from anything. Yet although equipped with powerful fins for propulsion, the tail is actually slender and streamlined.

Jake eases himself forward, and just as he grasped the large turbot, now he intends to tackle the conger. With a mighty heave of his crusher claw, he crashes right through the firm tail with a hard-solid crunch, shattering the vertebrae. Instantly, the eel flexes and thrusts forward with full power, yanking himself free, and charges into the open sea. Although severely damaged and bleeding the end of the tail remains firmly attached by the intricate series of muscles and spiny bones attached to the fins.

It will be some while before the wounded conger will return to the hole. He propels around in confusion, weaving through the tangled kelp and oar weed with his kinked tail and swollen jaw shattered during his confrontation with Trevor the bull crab some while before.

Jake then lumbers towards the unguarded entrance and out into the sea garden before him. Alone and aged, he seeks a new lair as he has no desire to share a nest with a conger. He travels the ledges and seaweed-carpeted rocks until he finds a slab of iron that has broken from the wreck. It is wedged in a corner of a gully, making a deep dark retreat with a concealed entrance. He chases several fiddler crabs from the depths and the resident gobies and rocklings move cautiously aside.

The floor is coated with fine silt that has settled over several months and it has the familiar scent of another lobster who resided here before moving on. With his great claws, he pushes mounds of silty sand to the entrance, and makes a deep scoop in which to settle. The mound of fresh sand he has cleaned out is a sign that confirms he is in residence. Most of the time, he rests with his claws imbedded in the sand at the entrance to ward off intruders.

For many days, he sits and waits yet nothing passes his new lair. The stumps of his feeler and his fine small antennae keep track of all movement. He senses another lobster approaching and edges forward to observe. It could well be another bull to challenge him for his comfortable new home.

Slowly and cautiously, a pair of fine red whiskers probes the mound of sand, just like a spider examining its web.

Jake watches as they quiver delicately in the dark.

Through the murk comes a cream-edged pair of claws mottled with fresh pale blue. Then the proboscis and eyes are revealed, showing that this is a young female called Sapphire who has just completed her second hatch of microscopic babies.

She sees Jake's impressive claws that could crush her body with one snatch. Yet undaunted Sapphire tickles them with the fine antennae and slowly paces forward, one of her eight spindly legs at a time, and inches closer to Jake's dangerous armour. He remains motionless as she feels his huge carapace and gnarled beak. With a few quicker steps, she lifts herself over his claws and disappears into the sanctuary behind him. She sees he is alone and of great age, having carried his armour for many seasons. He would be a suitable partner for her. She has eggs inside her body awaiting fertilisation by a male.

Delicately, she emerges from the depths of the hole and settles down alongside him. He passes his stumpy feelers over her carapace from her sharp nose to her fanned tail. She senses he has accepted her, so they can live together. Soon, her body will be ready to leave its old shell. She will then be soft, and in condition to mate with Jake.

When her shell hardens and she has fed sufficiently, she will produce eggs that will be attached and held under her tail for many months. Eventually, they will hatch into tiny crustaceans, a few of which will eventually grow into adult lobsters and sustain this ancient specie, the fascinating *homarus gammarus.*

And so the story of Jack the conger and Matilda the lobster has come to its sad conclusion. But life will carry on in a never-ending cycle for all the creatures and plants that live below the tides. It is a brutal world under the sea and lobsters are certainly one of the most aggressive species of all.

They are highly- territorial and cannibalistic. Juveniles will be eaten by the larger, particularly when they cast their shells. But the power in the claws of a large lobster can easily shatter the hard exoskeleton of smaller ones, so little is safe.

The conger eel is one of the most powerful creatures that lives on the sea bed—the equivalent of an anaconda in a tropical forest. It will inhabit wrecked ships and any natural ledge or hole in the rocks place that makes a suitable refuge and ambush point. Its voracious appetites leave no creature safe, particularly crustaceans when soft and vulnerable. Joe's prediction of the conger eel devouring a soft lobster is a true reflection of the facts of the brutal life that continues on the sea bed below the flowing tides.

Aggressive Conger Eel

Chapter Ten

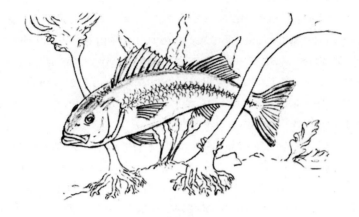

Bass

Reconciling the Future

Jason is standing above the shelving rocks of Blackledge. The tide slowly recedes as the tip of the wreck begins to break through the swirling eddies of the glassy ebbing sea. The rocks are dappled with dozens of sea birds, mainly gulls, oyster catchers and turnstones, that scurry in search of food as the rocks expose. This tells him he is the first person to be there that day, particularly at the pool where he missed the lobster the day before, the one that the unpleasant couple subsequently caught. The ebb is a foot lower, so he hopes to find several new crab and lobster holes as described by Joe.

Suddenly, a flurry of birds takes to the air in a cacophony of calls. Coming around the corner from the far bay is a young man in his late teens with unkempt blonde hair. He is wearing canvas work trousers ripped off untidily above the knees and a dirty grey tee shirt with several holes. He clutches a short stick and carries a sack on his shoulder.

Unmistakably, he is the farm boy who wore blue shorts on the previous tides; and also the one who was standing back from the other boys who tormented Joe two weeks before. Jason looks at the almost invisible mark on his arm caused by the blow intended for the ruffians.

Jason feels very alone as the boy stamps his way through the pools heading directly for him. He is uncertain what to do but feels sure some conflict might ensue. He is horribly aware that his relatively puny form is a marked contrast to the rough strength of the oncoming boy, who has a tanned unwashed face with fair stubble on his chin and a small moustache. It is too late for Jason to retreat; hesitantly, he stands his ground although he is shaking inside.

Jason starts prodding his hook into a corner of a shallow pool while his mind flashes back to incidents at school. He has to stand his ground. He runs his net through the weed in the pool and to his surprise it comes up containing a pile of green sea lettuce and a few jumping large prawns. Deftly, he grabs them and deposits into his haversack. *That was neat,* he thinks, and it boosts his confidence. He carries on working his net through the weedy pool.

'What you doing here again, kid?' the boy growls.

'Come to search for prawns, but the tide's not out very far,' Jason replies, determined to keep his voice steady, knowing the boy saw him catch something.

'Won't get to the wreck today,' the boy retorts.

'There are plenty of good prawns in these pools here, and I'm hoping to find some crabs as well,' Jason says calmly, still masking his anxiety. 'And what have you caught already?'

'Looking for bait, soft crab for fishing. My old man had plenty of crabs from those rocks yesterday,' the boy says, pointing in the direction of the next headland. 'Now wants to catch some bass; beautiful fish y'know. My family are all experts at bass fishing. Grandfather was the top bass fisher round here. It's best fish to eat too. Ever tried to fish for bass? Best fishin' there is. Now have to get bait back for pop. But ya should try. My kid brother is ya age and he caught a five pounder on the last tides. Get y'self a rod. I'll show ya,' he takes in Jason's nervous demeanour and smiles.

Tentatively, Jason smiles too. 'That would be nice, but I have to go home at the weekend as school starts next week.'

'School, huh? Didn't do me any good. I quit at fourteen t'work on the farm. Outdoor life's much better.'

Jason sighs. 'You're right. I love the outdoors, and coming here, but I have no choice; I have to go back.'

'Well, if you come back again, get a fishin rod, and I'll teach ya to catch bass!' the boy says with another smile that makes Jason relax a little more. 'An look at this!' he pulls a handful of black silky seaweed from his bag. 'Lava! My ma cooks this, it's delicious and good for ya. Gives strong muscles,' he says, flexing his arms. 'Feel this, kid!' he pulls up his shirt arm to reveal his biceps. 'Solid! Muscles make a man, mun, feel it!'

Cautiously, Jason reaches forward and grips the firm muscle, full of admiration for its sheer strength.

'You want t'pick some and try. Plenty in the gullies. Pick it clean, wash it in a pool and wring dry. Then boil heck out of it for a few hours. It's real tasty.'

'I'll be back in the summer holidays, I hope,' Jason says in a more confident voice. 'I'll certainly try some then, and I want to try bass fishing as well.'

'Well, come and find me, 'ere on tides—or East End Farm, call there. Ask for Cliff. Must get on now, see ya in summer!' he turns to walk away.

Jason then summons all the courage he can and calls, 'Excuse me asking, but do you mind if I, if you can tell me...' he hesitates a few seconds, 'please, why were you, well the others with you, well um...why were they teasing the old man by the paper shop, about two weeks ago. He is very old and frail, very frail?' he looks directly at Cliff who glares straight back at him.

Cliff squats down and looks out to sea then back at Jason. 'I didn't think anyone was around, how did you hear of it?' he barks.

'Well, I was walking up the hill and saw it, from a distance though. It upset me, he is an old man.'

'Kid, I don't like it either. I remember my gramps when he was old. I was the only one who visited him. Nobody else bothered. They only went to his house to steal anything they could. They virtually left him to starve. It was only a kind lady who lived nearby who fed him. But with that old guy, there has been a family feud for years. My elder brothers and cousins loathe him. There used to be horrible confrontations if they met in the village, in the pub, on the rocks fishin', wherever. I was very young and don't know much of it, but they will never forget. He was very strong and quick tempered when younger, apparently,' he pauses and stands up and stares at the wreck. 'Sorry, kid, that's life in a small village. It's like too many foxes or badgers trying to live in the same woods…heck, I must go, old man will be waiting! He wants to fish the tide as it turns. So long, lad. Maybe see you in the summer,' he pats Jason on the shoulder, grabs his sack and trudges briskly across the rocks and ascends the cliff to the coast track.

Jason watches him as he gets to the top. He has a positive feeling about having stood his ground as it led to a good exchange between the two of them. Cliff turns and waves to Jason, and he gestures back enthusiastically.

Can he be the same person? He was with the bullies who were mocking Joe, Jason thinks. But then he definitely was the one who kept out of the taunting. So perhaps he's not nasty like the others. He did seem to be sincere. Maybe he *was* disgusted by their treatment of Joe, but could not really say so.

Jason knows he would never forgive the others, but the more he thinks about it, the better Cliff seems. The prospect of learning to fish for bass is certainly exciting, filling his mind with a host of fresh ideas. He looks out at the wreck and in the few minutes the water has dropped away to reveal the beds of serrated wrack washing in the gentle waves. He thinks about finding some beautiful crabs.

He strips to his swimming trunks, and puts his clothes in the usual cave. Then he jumps waist deep into a pool, and begins scratching under the crannies with his hook. He plunges into a gully, totally submerging himself, then springs out shaking the water off his head like a young otter. He wades across another pool chest deep to reach an overhang where he spots a large round-shelled crab tucked into a recess.

He clasps it recklessly and shaking like a terrier pulls it away, the motion causing him to slip backwards under the water. Even so, he clings to it resolutely as he splashes back to his feet. He cheers to himself as he holds the fine cow crab aloft, then covers it with seaweed and dumps it into his haversack Then he jumps into a narrow water-filled creek, lunging in joy into the saline wavelets as he reaches for a hole he knows should hold another worthwhile crab. He wriggles the occupant out but, assessing it's just undersized, casts it out into the deep water like an outside fielder.

He is far out on the rocks, as close to the wreck as he can get. He contemplates swimming across the swirling water to claim it like a mountaineer reaching a peak, but caution prevails as he calculates the speed of the flow of the silky water. Instead he turns and looks back to the cliffs. He is gloriously alone with not a single person in sight. He darts with new-found confidence and the agility of a gazelle to scour other rocks as they emerge on the ebb. Soon, he has found a further three crabs and holds his haversack high to feel the weight of the catch.

By now, the gully where he lost the lobster to the self-satisfied couple is well out of the water, and he leaps across the fifty yards to the spot. He anticipates cloudiness in the pool—Old Joe said a second lobster was often likely when a hole has been occupied. Stealthily, he creeps into the pool and up to the hole. But as he slides the hook into the depths, a large fiddler crab scurries out clutching its mate under its tail. He knows from Joe that such a crab would not cohabit with a lobster, so there is nothing else there. He watches the red-eyed, velvet-backed creature swim away to find some refuge under some dangling seaweed.

The last stretch of rock yields one further crab, making a reasonable catch, but he doesn't see a whisker of a lobster in any of the holes he finds, and shrugs, a tad disappointed. He gives up for the day accepting that every venture onto the rocks will have its successes and failures. Still, he does have some very fine crabs.

As he dries his body, he looks at the pale hazel colour of his thighs that the sunshine and sea-salty air of the rocks have brought about on the fine days of his holiday. It contrasts starkly with the white of his skin that has been hidden by his trunks.

He cannot ever imagine acquiring such a colour in his home town. For him, it symbolises the freedom he's relished over his holiday, yet it's something he knows has to come to its inevitable end, and soon.

While he dresses, he sees two men in heavy clothes shuffling over the rocks bearing fishing rods and large bags of tackle. They set up their camp a hundred yards from him as they prepare their afternoon fishing. But Jason knows his own time is over and slowly, he climbs up the track to the cliff path. He stops and gazes at the wreck and the flooding tide. He licks his forearm, ingesting the sea-salt tang, and realises it's the last time he will taste this for some while. Slowly, almost reluctantly, he walks along the path. Frequently, he looks back at the rocks where he has enjoyed so much freedom and fun in solitude over the last three weeks.

Suddenly, Abby appears from around a corner, running towards him. She wears white tennis shorts and a matching shirt and clutches a racquet.

'Cor, matey, you have a nice full bag there; how many you caught? Had to play tennis with a friend, and the game went on and on. Was hoping to get to see you on the rocks. Sorry.'

'Oh, don't worry, but I did miss you. Caught five crabs! Didn't see a lobster, but there we are. Can't get one every time, I suppose,' he replies in a bouncy tone.

'Didn't get near your secret hole, I guess?'

'We won't get there until the late summer tides. I hope I will be able to get down for those. It's up to my parents, and Aunty and Uncle; but I really hope so. You'll be here, won't you?' Jason says.

Abby beams. 'Right on, it will be the summer vacation till mid-September. I'll be waiting for you. Got t'see if Jack and Matilda are still there; should be safe under the waves until then. Let's hope.' Then she rummages in her pocket and pulls out a small booklet with a green cover and holds it out to Jason. 'Here, for you. I found it in the bookcase and my uncle said I could have it. But I want you to enjoy it, I think you will.'

Jason looks at the cover and is somewhat taken back. The Ecology of a Rock Pool by RR Fowell. His face lights up. 'For me, are you sure?'

Abby nods at him and beams warmly.

'Oh thanks; it's so kind of you!' Quickly he flicks through the pages.

'It has all the Latin names, so you can be a real boffin and show everyone how clever you are. Mind you, I'll be testing you next time we meet. Must learn every one!' Abby smiles at him.

'I'll treasure this, I really will!' Jason enthuses. 'I'll write to you, I promise!' he gives her a gentle hug and a small kiss on her cheek.

'Sure thing, we'll be pen pals for a few months. But you must write back within seven days, or our pact will break. Works both ways. Can you keep to it?'

'Yes, definitely,' he smiles. She kisses him gently on the cheek and smiles too and they set off happily on their way back to Longbeach.

Blennie

The last time they will meet on this holiday will be in Sunday church the following morning. Jason is due to catch the one o'clock train home so will have little time to spare as first he will have to catch the bus to the station. He hopes to see Old Joe before he departs and knows his time is ebbing away.

He spends most of the remaining afternoon and evening writing diligently in his room. Charles and Gertie assume he is checking over his homework. Then he appears in time for his final supper: his favourite ham and parsley sauce, with mashed potatoes, and spring cabbage flavoured with mint from the garden.

'I am going to miss food like this, particularly the vegetables. But everything you've cooked, Aunty, has been utterly delicious. And this is too!' he says sincerely. 'Thank you both for such a wonderful time, Aunty and Uncle.'

'It has been wonderful for us too, isn't that so, Charles?' Gertie says, saddened that his stay is over.

'Couldn't agree more,' says Charles, patting Jason's shoulder for a moment.

'I feel I have found out so much about nature, particularly during the time searching the rocks. The life there is fascinating, but it's only exposed for such a short time to observe before the sea comes in again. Joe said it takes a lifetime to appreciate it fully, and you never stop learning, even then,' Jason sighs. 'And I'm sure he is right.'

'He certainly knows that better than anyone. Well, darling, your next visit will be an opportunity to add to *your* knowledge,' Gertie says, as Charles nods in agreement.

Aunty is to pack up the crabs of the last catch in lots of wrappers to insulate them for their journey back to the Midlands. Jason wants to surprise his parents with a supper of fresh crab. In his time, he has become very adept at preparing and dressing the catch. He's a little disappointed not to be taking a lobster as well, but no such luck. That's fishing; something that he's learning quickly.

Jason keeps writing late into the night until he can feel his eyelids drooping. He hears Aunty going to bed, shortly followed by Charles. He has two neat small stacks of paper at his side, one of which he folds and puts in an envelope which he seals and marks 'Abby'.

In his Sunday suit, Jason marches with Charles and Gertie into Church long before most of the congregation arrives. They position themselves to have a clear view of the altar and all who enter. Silently, Jason kneels and prays for over five minutes, then sits and gazes at the seascapes and models of boats in the windows. The main seats in the nave are taken quickly and Joe is assisted to a place close to the door.

Abby arrives with a group of friends and they sit towards the front. The service is Matins at eleven o'clock with just four hymns, but Jason gives his full voice to each. He chooses to ignore the few who turn to look at him, particularly the unsmiling lady who unnerved him before.

As the service concludes, he makes his way outside to await Abby and Joe. Clutching the envelope, he is on tenterhooks with anticipation. He knows there is a harsh end to his tale but feels sure she will appreciate that it's the raw truth of sea life. He sees Abby first. She is with four other girls yet she splits from them to speak to him.

'Well, I guess it's goodbye for a while,' he says in a tense voice. 'But here, this is for you. I hope you like it as I wrote it for you,' he hands her the bulging envelope. She looks surprised but then prises open the seal and sees it's his handwriting on the pages inside.

'Mean you wrote this for me? I must keep it safe. I can't wait to read it. I'll keep it and return to you.'

'Don't worry, I've a copy for myself. I wrote it out twice, so both are identical.' Inside he knows she will be saddened by parts of his story, as he is. 'It's called *The Tale of Jack and Matilda*; you can guess some of it, I but hope also it reveals some of their secrets!' He knows that the end of his tale is perhaps rather a shock, but knows that it reflects reality, both from what he has read, and what he has learned from Joe.

'Ha, a beautiful lady and an old bully together, eh?' she laughs. 'I'm really intrigued, Jason. Thank you.'

For a moment, he looks a little deflated. He is a little unsettled by the word "bully" as already his mind is thinking of his return to school, where he will no doubt face all the bullies again. Once more, he sees a sea of faces all laughing at the only boy to be caned in front of the school, a stigma he will never shake off. He can see the face of the bully and recalls his retaliation, and then the humiliation of having to face the headmaster, and then his punishment which he felt was so unjust.

But his expression changes as he knows that the challenges he dealt with here and the success on the rocks over the last few weeks have given him a new inner strength and confidence to face what is to come in school. As he considers his improved situation, he breaks into a smile that induces Abby's face to light up, and she smiles back at him.

'I'll appreciate this for sure; guess my mates wouldn't believe lots of it; perhaps me neither, but how imaginative of you! Now, I'll write ma first letter once I've read this. I'll hide it under my pillow and think of you. And Jason, learn to like school! Be yourself. Guess you've learnt a lot on this stay; done things lots of others haven't done and never will. So tell the tales to all: show your new confidence and even your lovely tanned body. It'll make them admire you; and anyone who upset you, well just ignore them, ignore them. Remember, ignore them!'

She gives him a gentle peck on the cheek and he blushes. She turns and trots back to her friends, turning to wave as she goes through the churchyard gate.

Jason runs down the grass verge to catch up with Old Joe, who as before is assisted as he shuffles towards the waiting car.

Jason calls out, hoping he will hear, 'Mr Joe, it's Jason. I hope you liked the crab.'

The old man turns slightly, taking a deep breath. 'Beautiful, fresh as a daisy, tasting of the waves; sweet as the sea spray in the spring. Thank ye, lad,' he puffs feebly, a friendly smile spreading across his wrinkled face.

'Sadly, I go back home today. But I do hope to visit again in the summer holidays,' Jason says, lifting his voice. 'And I hope it will be on the spring tides, so I will bring you another cow crab for your supper, in August.'

'That would be fine, ahhh…if I'm about still, cos the old clinker boat's nigh full o' water, so we'll see…' And Joe turns and shuffles along, with a helping hand on each elbow, towards the car that will take him home. Both of the men turn and nod to Jason, who smiles back and waves.

Suddenly, Jason looks down, thinking of Joe's parting words. Then he trots after Joe as he is helped into the car.

'You *will* be here, I know, I know. And I'd love to hear more of your secrets of the low tide; it's made this holiday for me. It opened my eyes to something I never imagined before.'

'Good, lad! Yet ye've a lot to learn; takes a lifetime to know it all, just as everything in life; never stop learning and listening, cos never know what ye'll pick up. Keep diligent and keep learning.' With a muffled grunt, Joe flops into the seat and closes his eyes.

'Thank you, young man, he really appreciated it. I suppose it takes him back to his best days; really kind of you to think of an old man, really kind. We must get him back now. Thanks again. Bye, lad,' says one of the men to Jason, and then they drive slowly away.

Charles and Gertie call to Jason and they walk home. Straight away, Jason goes upstairs, changes from his suit into his school uniform, then brings the fully-packed case downstairs He carries his case and walks with Charles and Gertie to the bus station on the village square. Charles has with him a cardboard box tied with sisal to make a handle. It contains the crabs that Jason carefully wrapped in grease-proof bread paper, with an outer layer of newspaper to keep them cool during the journey home. Jason has stored his hook and net in the outside toilet at Charles and Gertie's where they will be dry and safe. He climbs onto the double-decker bus and slides the case and box under the stairs. Then he turns to look at his uncle and aunt and a tiny tear runs down his cheek.

'Thank you, it's been wonderful, I've relished each day, and every meal, and cannot thank you enough for everything. I hope I can come back in the summer holidays. Is that all right?'

'Jason, you're more than welcome any time, it's been lovely having you, so of course you must come again,' Gertie says, wiping Jason's cheek with a small lace handkerchief. 'And remember, darling, learn to appreciate your studies. Literature, poetry, Shakespeare, for one day I'm sure you'll be a writer yourself; I can see you will be. And as for the sciences, now you are beginning to understand the wonders of nature, you will relish these as well. And please, don't forget to write to your Aunt Gertie and Uncle Charles. We do hope to see you in the summer, darling,' she tucks the handkerchief into her blouse pocket.

'Ye're the son we never had, eh Gertie?' Charles says then smiles at Jason. 'I'll have ye diggin' the garden in the summer, eh, lad. So ye can grow the vegetables as well as catch the crabs. Ye'll be welcome!'

Jason holds his right hand high, smiling, then climbs the stairs to take a seat at the front of the bus.

As the bus swings around in the square, both are waving from the pavement. Jason beams and waves back as they disappear from sight. He gazes across the bay where the sea is far in the distance. There are patches of black weed-covered rock and wide areas of dull-brown wet sand. Many seabirds, in large flocks or individually, are busy foraging for food.

Far away, a large black Labrador charges across the sand, splashing through shallow pools and sending showers of water high into the air.

It sets a group of curlews into the air with a loud warble of whistles and shrieks as their brown and sand plumage rustles in the breeze. Undaunted, the dog prances in freedom after another small flock as its insatiable enthusiasm drives it on.

'Lucky dog! What a place to live,' Jason sighs out loud, as he watches the freedom of the dog's life on the sands.

As the bus slowly rounds the sweep of the bay, it passes a corner, where on the pavement a group of young men looks familiar. The quick glimpse of them makes him shudder as he's sure they are the ones he saw on the rocks and who teased Old Joe so unkindly. He cannot see if Cliff is with them or not. Then before he can think any more about them, they disappear from sight.

The bus pulls into a stop and a few people alight while others get on. It then swings away from the bay into a wide road with shops and houses on either side. Jason goes to the window on the other side and stretches in vain to attempt one last view of the sea. He turns to go back to his seat, but immediately, his eyes fix on one figure sitting across the aisle. It is the lady with ginger hair. Slowly, almost deliberately, she turns around until she is staring at him face on. Jason freezes and tries to look down, but the set expression on her face makes it impossible.

'You are the boy I have seen in church, aren't you?' she says in a soft voice with school-mistress's intonation. 'I've seen you there, and heard your singing! The entire congregation could hear your voice.'

'Yes, I try my best, I love the hymns and psalms,' Jason replies as calmly as he can, despite his nervousness.

'Where are you from?' she commands.

'I've been staying with my uncle and aunt, but now I'm going back to the Midlands. But I do hope to come down again in the summer,' he replies, keeping his voice steady.

'You should come and join the church choir next time,' she says with an unexpected slight smile that makes Jason unwind a little. 'My brother-in-law is the choirmaster. They practise every Monday evening at six. Go to the vestry and ask for Mr Maldwyn Williams. Say Miss Mullet—that's me—has sent you. Don't forget. I'll keep an eye out for you in August.'

Jason gives a rather surprised smile. She is not the dragon he feared after all! 'Thank you very much indeed, Miss Mullet. I would really like that. My name is Jason, and I'll certainly do that. I shall look forward to it.'

'You should have a while before your voice breaks,' she nods. 'And now my stop is coming up, so I'll be away. Now don't forget—Monday evenings, Mr Williams, choirmaster.' She heaves herself from the seat, nods once more at Jason and descends the stairs.

Jason breathes a sigh of relief. What he saw as criticism and disapproval was no more than detached assessment. The thought of singing in the choir in August really lifts his spirits. Then he leans back and wriggles his pocket notebook from inside his jacket. He concentrates on the sketches of the crab and lobster holes and adds a few lines to enhance the detail. In the middle is the copy of the story he gave to Abby. He reads a page and smiles contently to himself.

Before he knows it, the bus stops at a small train station close to the sea front, a few miles from the town on the far side of the bay. He climbs a short flight of steps to the entrance where a uniformed man checks his ticket and directs him to the eastbound platform. A few people are sitting on the wooden benches awaiting the arrival of the mid-afternoon train. He sits and reads his notebook for a few minutes, then, in the distance, he can hear the panting of the steam engine far inland.

Trees are coming into full foliage and surround the track beyond the station. From the platform, he can just get a tiny glimpse of the sea to the south. The mesmeric rhythm of the train gets closer and closer until most people are standing in anticipation. Suddenly, with a great long honk from the horn and a billow of puffing steam, the train rumbles from the trees, passes through a yellow gorse-brightened cutting, and comes slowly to a halt with a final hiss from the brakes.

Jason strides along the platform, his case and package firmly gripped, and climbs aboard Carriage D where his seat is booked. He hoists his case, which also contains his satchel, and the box containing the crabs onto the netting-covered rack above his seat, takes off his jacket and settles alongside the window.

After a sharp blow of the station master's whistle, just like a referee calling time, the mighty engine sends out a huge puff of steam, and the first deep thump from the pistons sets the locomotive slowly into motion. The pounding of the engine gets quicker and the eight carriages rumble along the curving track heading through the trees and on towards a rolling meadow and open blue sky. The rhythm of the engine, the thrust of the pistons, the puffing steam from the chimney, all begin to sing in harmony as the track suddenly breaks from a tree-shrouded cutting onto a slight embankment.

The view of the bay to the south spreads across the window where Jason appreciatively stares at the wet yellow sands, with white-crested wavelets gently washing the shore and the shimmering blue of the sea beyond.

The track soon follows the edge of the shore, nestling in the sandy dunes that in places hide the view. The harmony of the throbbing engine creates a quicker and quicker verse of repeating sounds, and Jason sings to himself: 'Lobster, crab, prawn, shrimp; lobster, crab, prawn, shrimp,' he repeats it continually with the pounding of the engine as it speeds along the periphery of the bay.

Then, with a long and high screech of the engine's whistle, the locomotive's pace begins to retard and the speed diminishes. Gradually, the train swings to the north on a great curve heading inland, and Jason's treasured view of the sea changes to one of rolling hills studded with factory chimneys, rows of cottages and conical coal tips. He will not see the sea again for a while and he looks back longingly, as it will be months before there is any hope of returning.

He stands on his seat and rummages his *Pocket Guide to the Seashore* from his case, and looks up bass in the fish section. He reads avidly about the handsome-looking fish and the many others that inhabit the coastline. He drifts into deep thought of the rocks where Jack and Matilda share a hole together. He imagines the many other fish swimming in the swirling water and all the crustaceans scurrying amongst the rocks.

In his drifting mind, he pictures many new expanses of rocks yet to be searched, and numerous gullies to fish for bass on the flooding tide. He sees himself casting a line out to the choppy sea and anticipates that, at any second, a bass will take his bait. He imagines his trio of a catch: several large brown crabs, a two-pound lobster as blue as the midnight sky in summer, and a large slate-backed, silver-bellied five-pound bass caught in the rapidly flooding seas. He has caught them all from one day's tide, and they are proudly laid out amongst glistening deep-green seaweed ready for a proud photograph.

He drifts in and out of dreamy sleep travelling the imaginary shoreline, singing along with the ever-changing chant of the locomotive. It crosses the countryside, taking inclines with a heavy stolid throbbing from the hard-working pistons.

'Conger! Conger! Conger!' he chants along with the deep repetitive sounds.

The engine's hard work is then rewarded as it cruises down the slope to a wide valley. He sings to the quick tune of the whirring wheels as they accelerate, speeding the carriages on their way.

'Catching bass in the chafing waves, catching bass in the chafing waves,' he hums along to himself, longing for the time when he is heading back to the beautiful coastline again.

Eventually, he wills himself to a fidgety, anxious sleep.

Silently, he sings to the sound of the waves as the rhythmic steam engine chants in his mind, just like the changing moods of the turning tides.

Five hours later, the locomotive finally approaches the station of his home town. As he pulls his luggage from the rack above, he stares out of the window into the darkness of the falling night. His imagination momentarily drifts far away, back to the coastline he now loves. The full moon is diffused over the lazy sea that glistens in the dark of the night. Slowly, his mind dives below the high tide, down several fathoms to the undulating rocks where dancing seaweed shimmers as it reaches high towards the milky lunar light.

He searches for the familiar shapes of the rocks where his favourite crab and lobster holes are lost in the confusion of the swirling of the depths. Distorted images become clearer; the wreck towers above him and he glides towards his secret hole. He sees Jack with his huge head and yellow eyes resolutely guarding his lair. Matilda, with her midnight-blue carapace and bright red feelers, snuggles alongside him, both residing happily in their sea garden, and wonders if his story of the two will actually happen. He smiles hoping that it will not, certainly not before he returns to the rocks and to the secret hole again.

He calls to them through the window, misting the glass; as their images disappear, he prays for their safety until he returns. He longs for the days of the summer when he will be back to search the seashore and relish the secrets of the tides once more.

'I'll be back,' he says to himself. 'I know I will!' he smiles. 'I look forward to confronting many new challenges and more exciting adventures on the seashore.'

The End

More tales of Jason's adventures will follow...

'I have been taught the script of the stones, and know the tongue of the wave.'

Vernon Watkins

'I'm going to paddle once a day from now on...I'm going to go down to the sands every evening and have a good paddle. I'm going to splash about and get wet up to my knees. I don't care who laughs. When I wake up in the morning, there's nothing to look forward to...now, I'll be able to wake up and think: This evening I'm going to splash about in the sea.'

Ray in 'Portrait of the Artist as a Young Dog'
Dylan Thomas

'It was my thirtieth birthday to heaven
Woke to my hearing from harbour and neighbour wood
And the mussel pooled and the heron
Priested shore
The morning beckon
With water praying and call of seagull and rook.'

'October'
Dylan Thomas

Author's Afterword

Fishing on the coast of Britain has changed considerably over the last half century and more, as have the attitudes towards all wildlife, exploitation and conservation. In this time, there has been disastrous over-fishing at all levels and stocks of many species depleted. More recently, a host of conservation measures have been brought in together with local fishery by-laws, aiming to control stocks. Shellfish have been subjected to high levels of fishing from potting, trawling, bait gathering and skin divers. Nonetheless, the edible crustaceans on the inter-tidal zone, once plentiful, are now more of a rarity, apart from invasive spider crabs that can appear in large numbers in the summer for a short time. The shortage of potential food on the intertidal zones has led to a decrease in the number of predators such as conger eels that inhabit these areas. Congers are caught by anglers and trawlers fishing in deeper water and some now appear in fishmongers.

Handling live seafood is now far more careful than some of the rough treatment in the past. There have been many different opinions on the most efficient and kindest way to cook crustaceans. In the early twentieth and again in the twenty-first centuries, research was commissioned to address this. Both reports concluded that immersion of the shellfish in boiling water is the most effective and humane method.

The gathering of wild birds' eggs is now illegal, but gull's eggs can be harvested in some areas. However, this is strictly controlled by licences and a very limited collection season.

Nevertheless, there is still much to observe on the coastline and on the shore at low tide. There are many species of seaweed to identify. In some areas, shrimps and rock prawns can be plentiful, and small rock-fish can be found in pools. Shore crabs and fiddlers can also be plentiful, but edible crabs and lobsters are all controlled by size limits that can vary from area to area.

Always check local regulations before removing anything from the shore. Observe sea life where it is rather than away from its environment.

A golden rule is always to leave the rocks as you find them. If looking under stones for life, be certain to return the stones to their original position exactly as they were. Not doing so interferes with the fragile eco-system: creatures that inhabit the underside of stones, rocks and boulders, where direct sunlight cannot reach, are very different from the flora and fauna that thrive on the light on the top-side of rocks.

Be careful going to any intertidal areas, particularly on the rocks, and check times and heights of tides. Where there is a large tidal range, take extra precautions and never try to race against the incoming tide. Keep in sight of the land and allow plenty of time to get back there. The sea comes in at a deceptive speed.

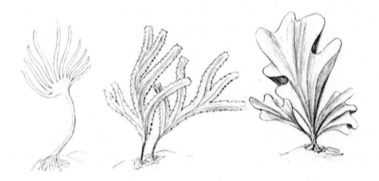

About the Author

C D Pressdee was brought up in Mumbles and attended Bishop Gore Grammar School in Swansea then the University of Wales, Cardiff where he read Economics, achieving a BSc (Econ) Hons degree.

Combining an interest in business with his lifelong passion, he started a seafood business exporting shellfish to most European countries.

His restaurant, The Oyster Perches, was the first in Swansea to gain entry to the *Good Food Guide* 1974 and was acclaimed for the use of local produce from Gower and South Wales. In late 1975, he opened the Drangway in the oldest area of Swansea (Drangway—a local word for a narrow lane). It had entries in *Michelin* with a Red M, the *Good Food Guide* and *Egon Ronay.*

In the late 1980s, he moved into marketing, undertaking many consultancies for the Enterprise Initiative, and became a registered consultant with Cranfield Business School. He undertook consultancies and food promotions throughout the UK and Europe. He staged food events in the European Parliament, Brussels; at the British Embassy, Paris; the International Celtic Festival in Lorient, Brittany and created a beach buffet party for 500 at the Mipcom Television Film Festival in Cannes.

In the 1990s, he took part in many assignments in Yemen, working on cultural exchanges with The British Council in Sana'a and Aden, and travelling through most areas of the country. Recently, he did an extended restaurant and hotel consultancy in Bali, Indonesia.

During this time, he also wrote regularly for the *Western Mail, Daily Post, The Times, Financial Times* and numerous other publications. He won a Glenfiddich Award in 1990 as Regional Writer of the Year.

His food books include: *Streetwise Cookery, Welsh Coastal Cookery, Food Wales* and *London Oyster Guide.*

Earlier works of fiction are: *Reflections of a Vampire* and *Devil's Recipe.*

He has taken part in numerous radio and television programmes and series including *Floyd on Great Britain* and *A Feast of Floyd.* He was a weekly contributor to *Streetlife* on BBC Radio Wales, and BBC Wales TV *See You Sunday,* and BBC2 *Summer Scene*, live from the Garden Festival in Ebbw Vale. He presented *Nightbites* on ITV and *Hedgerow Harvest* on UKTV.

Currently, he lives in Brighton, after 25 years in London. He continues to write and undertake consultancy in the food business both in the UK and abroad. He returns every summer to the Gower Peninsula.